DARK SUSPICION

When Aunt Jessica asks Caitlin to help run her art gallery while she is in hospital, Caitlin agrees. She hadn't bargained on having to deal with a series of thefts, however — or Jessica's insistence that Caitlin's new employer, Nicholas Millward, must be responsible. Nicholas is as ruthless as he is handsome, but would he really stoop to theft? And what can Caitlin do when she finds herself in the grip of a passion too powerful to resist?

SUSAN UDY

DARK SUSPICION

Complete and Unabridged

LINFORD
Leicester

First published in Great Britain

First Linford Edition
published 2014

A catalogue record for this book is available
from the British Library.

ISBN 978–1–4448–1867–3

Published by
F. A. Thorpe (Publishing)
Anstey, Leicestershire

Set by Words & Graphics Ltd.
Anstey, Leicestershire
Printed and bound in Great Britain by
T. J. International Ltd., Padstow, Cornwall

This book is printed on acid-free paper

1

Caitlin stared at the man standing across the room from her. His gaze was fixed upon her, just as hers was upon him. The steel grey eyes that were almost as familiar as her own were raking her keenly, the expression in them a disturbing one.

She'd hoped he wouldn't be here — had banked on the fact that he wouldn't be here, in truth. Yet, she should have known better than to rely on Nicholas Millward doing anything that could be even remotely described as predictable.

Nicholas Millward! The man who now owned Gallagher Electronics and who, she supposed, technically, would be her employer from this time on. He was the one who had forced herself and Patrick so ruthlessly into a corner but had suddenly seemed to relinquish

1

the fight and uncomplainingly paid Patrick's asking price for the company.

She shouldn't have come here. In the last few weeks, she'd seen too many people cowed and reduced to stammering wrecks by the man standing on the other side of the room to be under any illusions about the outcome of this encounter.

Nicholas Millward, she was quite sure, wouldn't be any more pleased to see her than she was to see him. What should she do? Her instincts urged her to get away as fast as her legs would carry her but her sense of courtesy told her that she couldn't simply turn tail and run, not without some sort of explanation. And what could Nicholas do to her when all was said and done?

He had turned to his companion and said something. He was clearly going to come over and confront Caitlin, possibly to demand her reasons for being there. So be it. Nicholas Millward wasn't going to be able to accuse her of

cowardice throughout any future dealings that they might have. She'd stand
her ground and, just as she had in the
past few weeks, she'd take and deal
with whatever he decided to dish out.

Caitlin's thoughts returned to the
phone call that had summoned her here
to the village of Chegston, to the Orion
Gallery, to Aunt Jessica's bedside and
indirectly to the auction in this house
and this unwelcome confrontation with
Nicholas Millward.

* * *

'Caitlin. It's Jessica.'

'Aunt Jessica!' Caitlin exclaimed. 'Is
anything wrong?'

Her aunt had phoned her only the
previous week and, as in normal circumstances, she made a habit of only contacting
Caitlin once a month at the most.
Caitlin sensed trouble immediately.

'I'm afraid so. I'm ringing from
hospital, Caitlin. I've had a heart
attack.'

'Oh, my goodness!'

'Don't worry, dear. It was only a small one. The thing is, they want to keep me under observation for a while.'

'Understandably. Look, Aunt Jessica, I'll come straight away.'

'I knew I could rely on you, Caitlin. But,' her aunt murmured, 'this is all very difficult and I hate to ask you but, I actually need someone to look after the gallery for me.'

'Why can't David do it?'

'Well, to be truthful, dear, I do feel that David's rather young for the responsibility.'

Caitlin couldn't bring herself to argue with that. Jessica's son, and her cousin, was an extremely immature twenty-year-old.

'I was speaking to your mother last week,' Jessica went on, 'and she happened to mention that you're about to take some time off work.'

'Yes. It's meant to be a holiday, though, Aunt Jessica. I've been over-working and the doctor has ordered me to rest. Alan's booked us up for a fortnight in the Seychelles.'

'I hate to do this to you, Caitlin, but I don't know whom I can turn to.'

It was completely out of character for her normally strong-willed aunt to plead with anyone but that was undoubtedly what she was doing now.

'You sound worried, Aunt Jessica.'

'I am. I can't talk about it on the phone. Please, will you come, Caitlin? I really need you.'

'Well, if you put it like that, of course, I'll come.'

Caitlin had always been fond of her aunt, despite the older woman's forth-right and sometimes downright acid tongue. And as she said, who else had she to turn to?

Caitlin's parents had left England three years ago to live in the south of France, and remarked frequently that they had no intention of returning to cold, wet, dismal England.

Caitlin quite understood her aunt's reluctance to entrust her only son with her beloved art gallery. Much as Caitlin hated to think badly of anyone, David wasn't one of the world's most responsible people. He'd been a late addition to the family, and, as often happens in such cases, he'd been spoiled by both his parents.

'The only thing is, I know nothing about art,' Caitlin felt compelled to protest.

Jessica had hastened to reassure her niece.

'You don't need to. Everything's priced. All you have to do is sell the stuff — hopefully — and keep the place clean and tidy. I'll make it worth your while.'

'Aunt Jessica, there's no need for that.'

'Yes, there is. If you work for me I'll pay you whatever I would have had to pay someone else to do it.'

Caitlin replaced the receiver, her expression one of dismay. How was she going to tell Alan that she couldn't accompany him on holiday? They'd been due to fly out the day after tomorrow. Alan, usually the most placid of men, was going to be furious — understandably. But what else could she have done? Her aunt needed her more than Alan did, that was only too clear.

Absentmindedly, she checked her wrist watch. She'd have to tell Alan straight away. It was only fair. The trouble was that at three o'clock on a Monday he'd still be at work. She could ring him, she supposed. No, she couldn't tell him the sort of news she had for him over the phone. She'd go round to his flat on the dot of six.

So, promptly at six, Caitlin knocked on Alan's door.

She had decided on her way to his flat that the best way of handling this was to simply come straight out with it. No amount of preamble was going to make her decision any more acceptable.

'I'm afraid there's been a change of plans, Alan.'

His smile fled, leaving his expression

wary and uncharacteristically shuttered.

'What do you mean, a change of plans?'

'I can't go on holiday with you.'

'You're joking! We go the day after tomorrow.'

'I know.' She paused. 'It's Aunt Jessica. I've told you about her, haven't I?'

She was stalling, playing for time, but she just couldn't seem to help herself. She hated disappointing anyone, especially when it was someone she cared about.

Alan didn't speak, but she saw the way in which his mouth hardened and his eyes took on a hurt expression. She wished he'd say something — anything, shout at her, even. She stumbled on.

'She rang this afternoon. She's in hospital, you see.'

'No, I don't see. What's that got to do with you?' Alan's voice hardened.

'Well,' Caitlin said and attempted a bright smile, 'she's had a heart attack. The hospital want to keep her in and there's no-one to look after the gallery.'

'So she's asked you. Good, reliable, little Caitlin. What's wrong with her own son helping out? Why you?'

'David can't do it.'

She couldn't bring herself to tell Alan that David's own mother didn't trust him to manage things alone. It would seem disloyal.

'Did you tell her we were just about to go on holiday? That your doctor prescribed complete rest? How will you get that looking after a shop?'

His voice rose slightly as his anger and disappointment overtook his normally even temper.

'For goodness' sake, Caitlin, you've been showing all the symptoms of stress due to the pressure your blasted boss has been putting you under.'

'It wasn't Patrick, Alan, not entirely. I am his personal assistant, after all. He relies on me. If it hadn't been for the selling of Gallagher's . . . '

'But it was all due to that, and to the fight that went on with that Nicholas

Millward. You suffered due to the fact that Gallagher left so much of it to you to deal with while he went swanning off. It drove you to the brink of a nervous breakdown. The last thing you need now is more strain. Darling, listen to me.'

'No, Alan, I can't, I'm sorry. Aunt Jessica is the nearest family I've got now that my parents are so far away. I owe it to her. She needs me. She'd do the same for me, I know.'

'Would she, Caitlin? Are you sure of that? It strikes me that your family takes advantage.'

'That's quite enough, Alan. It's my business and I'm going.'

'If you put it before me and your own well-being, you can kiss goodbye to any future relationship between us.'

Suddenly, he looked like a little boy denied a promised treat. Caitlin contemplated the sulky lines of his face, the downward droop of the mouth. She sighed softly. This was precisely what she'd been afraid of.

'I'm sick and tired of always coming last with you, Caitlin,' he continued. 'There's always something or someone more important than me, isn't there? The last time we planned a week-end away, your parents turned up unannounced and dumped themselves on you. The time before that it was a friend in desperate need. People put on you, Caitlin! Can't you see that? And your precious family are the worst of the lot.'

'I'm sorry, Alan.' Caitlin's voice was firm now that she had made her decision. 'I can't let my family down, whatever you may think of me. Perhaps they do put on me from time to time, but isn't that what families are for? They'd all do exactly the same for me.'

'If you cancel this holiday, we're finished, Caitlin.'

'I'm sorry, Alan, I really am, that that's the way you feel.'

'Is that all you have to say? That you're sorry. For goodness' sake, Caitlin.'

'But I am sorry, Alan. You've been a

good friend to me. I'm sorry,' she said once again, spreading her arms helplessly.

As ineffectual as the words sounded, she didn't know what else to say. She turned to go and was surprised to feel the sting of tears. The last words she heard as she stumbled from the room were, 'Caitlin, please.'

Caitlin had wasted no time. That same evening, she had decided to drive to the village of Chegston to deposit her cases in her aunt's flat before going on to the hospital to see Jessica for herself.

Jessica always left a spare key with the people next door so it was an easy matter for Caitlin to collect it, unlock the Orion Gallery, turn off the burglar alarm and from there, ascend the steep flight of stairs to the living apartments above.

There was also a side door leading upstairs which her aunt had had installed when she first moved into the shop, in case she ever wished to rent the flat independently of the gallery, but on this occasion, Caitlin went through the shop.

Caitlin had visited Jessica and the gallery many times since Uncle William's death five years ago. Jessica had used a substantial part of the money he had left to buy the gallery from the elderly owner, Miss Hislop, and stock it. She also offered a picture-framing service which supplied her with what she called her bread-and-butter money.

Caitlin looked round now, eager to see what her aunt had in stock at the moment. Disappointingly, the walls were covered with what looked like relatively cheap prints. There were one or two original works by unknown artists but that was all. Caitlin, as she had told her aunt, was no connoisseur of art but, even so, the only painting of any worth that she could see was a small oil by Landseer.

She frowned, wondering why Jessica had insisted upon Caitlin coming to man the gallery. With only one painting of any value in stock, surely David, as immature as he was, could have been left in charge?

Although it was well past visiting time when she got to the hospital, a friendly nurse took her to her aunt.

'Caitlin,' Jessica said and held out a shaky hand to her niece. 'Thank you for coming, my dear. If you can hold the fort for a few days, I'm sure I won't be kept in here too long.'

'Don't worry about that, Aunt Jessica. I've got a whole month off work. I'm sure I could wangle longer if it becomes necessary. Patrick's very understanding.'

'Oh, I'm sure I won't be here that long.' Jessica attempted a rather tremulous smile. 'Providing, of course, that all these gadgets round me don't kill me off. Was your young man very disappointed about the holiday?'

'Just a little.'

Caitlin made light of Alan's anger. Jessica had enough to worry her already without having to fret about Alan's disappointment over the holiday as well. She crossed her fingers behind her back, telling herself that her small deceit was all in a good cause.

'You just do as the nurses tell you and I'm sure you'll soon be up and about. Now, what's been worrying you enough to make you enlist my help?'

'There have been a series of thefts from the gallery, Caitlin, and I need someone in charge who will remain on the alert.'

'Thefts? You mean of paintings? I noticed the bareness of the walls. Why haven't you mentioned it before?'

'I didn't want to worry anyone. I kept hoping that each one would be the last, but there have been three incidents now, in a little over eighteen months. The thing is, you see, I think I know who might be behind them. The trouble is, I've no evidence.'

'Have you told the police of your suspicions?'

'No. I told you, I have no proof. This

— this person has had it in for me ever since . . . '

'Ever since what? What's been going on, Aunt Jessica?'

'I shouldn't have mentioned it. Forget I said anything, Caitlin. As I said, I have no proof and the person to whom I'm referring has considerable standing hereabouts. No-one would believe me.'

'Are we talking about the owner of Pimpernel Gallery and Antiques by any chance?'

Jeremy something-or-other was his name, Jessica thought.

'Ssh, Caitlin. I don't want anything mentioned in here. You know what villages are like for gossip. If anything should get back to him . . . '

'So we are talking about Pimpernel Gallery.'

Caitlin didn't personally know this Jeremy but she knew enough about him to know that her aunt had disliked him for quite some time now, for a reason Caitlin had never been able to persuade

16

her aunt to disclose. But that she should suspect him of theft was a serious matter.

Jessica's voice was low as she went on.

'He's had it in for me ever since I bought the gallery. He came to see me, it must be two years ago now, and offered to buy me out. Clearly, although he didn't say so, his business had been suffering and he wanted to eliminate the competition. I refused his offer, even though it topped what I'd orginally paid for the place. Then, six weeks later, the thefts started. He's trying to drive me out!'

'You don't know that Aunt Jessica,' Caitlin chided. 'As you said, you have no proof.'

'I don't need proof, Caitlin. It's all too much of a coincidence. He makes me an offer, I refuse it, and soon after, paintings start to go missing, added to which,' she continued darkly, 'there hasn't been a single theft from the Pimpernel.'

'That does seem strange.'

'It's more than strange in my book. It adds up to one thing and one thing only. He's our thief, otherwise surely he'd have suffered the same thing. He has some valuable antiques in that shop, a lot of them quite small enough to slip under a coat.'

'What I don't understand in all this,' Caitlin said, 'is, if he was so keen to buy the gallery, why didn't he buy it from Miss Hislop before you did?'

'He tried but his initial offer wasn't as high as mine and Miss Hislop refused an auction. So by the time he'd come back with a higher offer, she'd already sold it to me. He has always said there isn't room for two galleries in the village, to which I always replied that it hadn't seemed to bother him when Miss Hislop was alive. Anyway, he said one of us would go bust and it certainly wasn't going to be him. Then, paintings started to go missing.'

'But you can't take his remarks made in the heat of the moment as evidence that he's responsible for the thefts. It's a very serious accusation to make.'

'I know, but he's out to ruin me. Take my word for it.'

'But you're insured against theft, aren't you?'

'Well, yes.'

'So, doesn't that make a nonsense of your theory that he's trying to ruin you by stealing paintings? All you have to do is claim back their value. Theft is inconvenient, I grant you, but it's hardly ruinous, is it?'

'Oh, never mind the technicalities of it, Caitlin.'

'I'm sorry. Go on.'

'The first painting that disappeared was one I outbid him for at an auction. It was worth quite a lot of money as were the next two that went.'

Caitlin frowned. 'If the paintings weren't all stolen at the same time but over a period of eighteen months, what makes you so sure that they were all stolen by the same person?'

'I'm not. I'm ninety-nine per cent

sure that his son stole the first one.'

'His son?'

'The day the first painting went missing, he'd been in the shop, snooping. It was after he'd gone that I noticed the painting had also gone.'

'How long afterwards?'

'An hour or so,' Jessica said but looked away suddenly.

'And who else had been in the gallery in the meantime?' Caitlin asked.

'Oh, one or two people.'

'So it could have been one of them, couldn't it?'

'It could have been, strictly speaking,' Jessica admitted reluctantly.

'Do you mean that someone, whoever it was, simply took a painting off the wall and walked out with it?'

Caitlin couldn't hide her incredulity.

'Must have done. It was only a small one, an oil, about ten inches by twelve. It could easily have been slipped under a jacket.'

'And was the son wearing a jacket?'

'Oh, yes. It would have been an easy

matter to slip it, frame and all, beneath his coat.'

'But they must know that you're insured against theft. Why not just set fire to the place? It would be a much more effective way of shutting you down.'

'Caitlin, not even Jeremy would go that far!' Jessica was clearly shocked at her niece's suggestion. 'I'm not as young as I used to be. I'm alone in the world. He's obviously hoping that all the hassle will force me into selling to him.'

'But you're not alone in the world, Aunt Jessica. You've David, me, my parents and Uncle William's family. I would hardly call that being alone, Aunt.'

'All right, so I'm not quite alone,' Jessica conceded. 'What I meant was, I'm without a husband to support me.'

'If you genuinely believe this son of his took the painting, how come you didn't see him do it?'

'I had to leave the shop for a few

moments, when the phone rang in the back office. It's no good you looking like that, Caitlin.' She'd clearly perceived Caitlin's disapproval. 'I never dreamed he would do such a thing. He seems so respectable.'

'Thieves often do, that's how they get away with it,' Caitlin remarked drily. 'Presumably you knew that he was this Jeremy's son?'

'Well, of course, I knew. But Nicholas Millward is . . . '

'Nicholas Millward! Nicholas Millward is the man we're talking about? The man you believe stole the painting?'

'Yes. Whatever is the matter with you?'

'It can't be the same man!' Caitlin argued, as much with herself as with her aunt. 'Describe him.'

'Well, he's tall, over six feet, I would have said. Powerfully built. Dark hair, almost black, eyes the colour of steel. Slightly hooked nose, aquiline, I suppose you'd call it, and bronze complexion. Good-looking chap, even I have to admit that.'

Caitlin was no longer listening to her aunt. It was him! It had to be. There couldn't be two Nicholas Millwards, not both fitting her aunt's description.

'Aunt Jessica, the man you've just described is the man who has just bought Gallagher Electronics — the man I've been doing battle with. He's my new boss.'

She had to persuade her aunt that there was no way that Nicholas would ever involve himself in anything as sordid as theft.

'He's a wealthy, much respected business man. Why, he could buy you out ten thousand times over and it would be a mere drop in the ocean to him. There's no way he would walk into a provincial art gallery and take a painting off its wall, not even to help his father.'

'Oh, I know all that, Caitlin. I'll grant you he's done very well to have reached the position he has by the age of thirty-four. His father couldn't have done it. But you're wrong in saying that he wouldn't do anything like that. That man would do anything. Don't doubt it for a moment, Caitlin.'

Aunt Jessica paused for a moment then continued, 'I've known Nicholas since he was a little boy. He's one of the most ruthless men alive. And that's the only reason I've held back from openly accusing him and his father. There's no telling what he would do to me. If you've had dealings with Nicholas Millward, then you'll know the truth of what I'm telling you. You keep well away from him, my girl, new boss or no. And that's the best advice I can give you.'

2

Caitlin left the hospital and drove back to the gallery feeling decidedly shaken. She'd had no notion that Nicholas lived here, in the same village as her aunt.

Jessica didn't need to tell her to stay away from Nicholas Millward. She had no intention of going anywhere near him, not while she was in Chegston at any rate. She'd have to see him soon enough once she was back at work, she imagined, although even that was doubtful.

He didn't usually involve himself in the day-to-day workings of his businesses from what she'd heard. Nicholas had kept Patrick on as general manager, saying that he knew as much about the running of the company as anyone. It had been the financial side of things that Patrick had failed at. With Nicholas at the helm, the company should soon be showing a profit again.

Jessica had told her that Nicholas owned a house in the village, a mile or two from his father's. Jessica had been unerring in her characterisation of Nicholas. He was utterly ruthless when it came to his own interests.

Caitlin knew that better than anyone. But was he ruthless enough to steal on behalf of his father? Never! And if Nicholas got wind of Jessica's accusations, suffice it to say, he would prove a formidable opponent. He was quite capable of bringing her aunt's business down.

Had he had any idea of her connection with Aunt Jessica, Caitlin wondered. It would explain the manner in which his gaze had frequently lingered upon her during their dealings together. The steely eyes had burned with a strange expression and, although she hadn't wished to admit to any such thing, it had excited her in a curious fashion.

The day after Caitlin's arrival in

Chegston, her cousin, David, turned up at the gallery.

'I don't know why Mum had to ask you to come,' were his first words. 'I could have run this place with one hand tied behind my back.'

'I think she wanted someone a little more mature, David,' Caitlin explained tactfully. 'A gallery like this is a considerable responsibility, especially in the light of the thefts. The insurance company might frown upon someone too young being left in charge if another painting should go missing. Mind you, there's not much of any value left.'

Her glance went to the Landseer, the one painting of any value.

'Well, if you want the truth, I'm not too sorry at not being asked to do it.' David glanced round the small gallery. 'Time can hang pretty heavy with nothing much to do and I'm not really into dusting picture frames. She told you about the paintings going missing then?'

'Of course. I had to be warned so I

can keep an eye out for any other potential shoplifters.'

'Did she tell you whom she thinks is behind it all?'

'Yes, Jeremy Millward and his son. The whole notion is preposterous, David.'

'Try telling Mum that.' The younger man shrugged.

'I have. She refuses to listen to me. Tell me, David, how did the other paintings go missing? I didn't want to press your mother for fear of getting her worked up against her doctor's orders.'

'One went the same way, lifted off the wall when no-one was looking.'

'And had Nicholas Millward or his father been into the shop on that occasion?'

'No, apparently not. Mum thought they'd probably paid someone else to do it, to avert suspicion from themselves, presumably.'

'And the third? How did that one disappear?'

'A break-in while Mum was out one evening.'

'But,' Caitlin exclaimed, 'the shop has an alarm. Did the thief manage to disarm it?'

'No. They drove a car through the front window and grabbed the painting right off the easel before anyone could get here.'

Caitlin frowned. She didn't like the sound of that. What was to stop someone doing the same thing while she was here alone?

'Your mother is wrong about the Millwards, David. I'm positive. I don't know Jeremy but I do know Nicholas.'

'You do?' David looked surprised.

'Yes. He's just bought the firm I work for. I really wouldn't advise you to broadcast your mother's suspicions. Nicholas Millward can be a very nasty customer if crossed.'

'Tell me about it,' David replied smartly.

Deciding it was time to change the subject, Caitlin asked, 'Where are you living now, David? Aunt Jessica said you'd left home but not where you'd gone.'

'I'm sharing with Donna. She's got her own flat, just up the road. She's an artist as well.'

'Oh, I see.'

'What if she brings a few of her paintings in to show you, with a view to the gallery buying them? You are in charge for the moment.'

'Oh, no. I don't think so, David. I couldn't go behind Jessica's back and make decisions of that sort.'

'No, I suppose not. Well, I'd better be going. I'm meeting Donna in half an hour.'

The next visitor to the Orion Gallery was a much more interesting one. It was none other than Jeremy Millward himself!

When he'd introduced himself, Caitlin hadn't been able to suppress the faint sensation of misgiving. Had he got wind of her aunt's suspicions about himself and Nicholas?

She needn't have worried, however. His manner couldn't have been more charming. There were no indications that his son took after him, either in looks or in character. Nicholas's father was a man almost as tall as his son. Caitlin would have gauged his age at sixty or thereabouts.

He possessed an air of distinction and was still a very attractive man.

'Don't look so anxious, my dear. I'm not here to snoop,' he reassured her. 'I've come armed only with an invitation.'

'Invitation?' Caitlin heard herself repeating.

Word of her arrival must have sped round the small village to induce Jeremy Millward to show up with an invitation.

'Yes. I thought you might not be very well acquainted with local folk in spite of your aunt having lived here for so long and as I'm holding a small party tomorrow night, I wondered if you'd like to come. It would give you the perfect opportunity to meet everyone in one go.'

'Oh, I don't really think . . . '

'I refuse to take no for an answer, I'll warn you now. Your aunt and I go back a long way. Has she never mentioned me?'

Caitlin felt herself stiffen.

'Um — not really.' He'd have a fit if he knew precisely what her aunt had said about him. 'Well, at least, only that you also have a gallery.'

'Yes, we are business rivals, if nothing else these days.'

The warm smile glinted at her again and Caitlin felt herself smiling in return.

'My other guests would never forgive me if our newest and prettiest resident weren't present at the party.'

'Well, I don't think I could be classed as a resident,' she protested. 'I'll be here for only a short time.'

'All right then, temporary resident.' He laughingly conceded the point. 'But even so, I'd never be forgiven if I were to hold a party and you weren't there. Please, say you'll come.'

'Oh, well, if you are so insistent, how can I refuse?'

There was nothing to fear by the sound of it. It would be a small gathering of elderly people, and it would seem churlish to refuse. It didn't sound like Nicholas's scene at all. That had been her chief fear, that he would be present, that and the prospect of her aunt's displeasure when she heard that her niece had been at a party given by the enemy.

She'd face Aunt Jessica when she had to. She was accustomed to her aunt's scolding. It no longer held any terrors for her. She'd learned long ago that Jessica's bark was considerably worse than her bite. Perhaps if Caitlin herself made the initial moves to heal the rift that seemed to have developed between her aunt and this charming man, Jessica, once she was recovered, would see the stupidity of her suspicions and follow suit.

It was a long shot that she was playing, knowing her aunt as she did, Caitlin admitted, but it was one that she felt she should try. She had realised, looking at Jessica lying in the hospital bed, just how alone the older woman was. With her husband gone and her son ostensibly leading his own life, apart from Caitlin, whom had she to turn to? A close friend nearby, such as Jeremy, could only be a bonus.

'Capital!' Jeremy exclaimed. 'Here's my card with my address and phone number. Come casual,' he added, 'for eight o'clock. We don't stand on ceremony in these parts.'

The next day being a Wednesday, the gallery didn't open, which ensured that Caitlin had plenty of time to select her most attractive outfit. She told herself, over and over, that her choice had absolutely nothing to do with the fact that Nicholas might possibly be present. She simply didn't want to disappoint his father and his friends.

But, nonetheless, her favourite pair of

linen trousers and matching blouse did wonders for her, as she had known it would, subtly emphasising her chestnut hair and green eyes.

When she was finally ready, she studied herself critically in the long mirror, at the same time giving her sleek hair its final brush. She walked out of the bedroom, flinging a soft, cashmere jacket over her shoulders as she did so in anticipation of a possibly chilly walk home later.

But, in marked contrast to the previous couple of days, the evening was sunny and still warm as she locked the side door that led directly up to the flat. It had rained earlier so everything had a freshly-washed smell, the leaves on the trees that lined the village's main street shining as they formed their lacework pattern against the evening sky.

She left the outskirts of the village and continued along the lane that would eventually lead her to Jeremy's home. The very air was scented, mainly due, she guessed, to the dog roses that were in abundance along the hedgerows.

She'd spent the better part of the day regretting her acceptance of the invitation and she regretted it even more when she saw the grandeur of the house confronting her. It stood at the end of a rhododendron-lined drive, its mullioned windows tinted gold by the lowering sun.

There was no shortage of money here, that was starkly evident. But whose money? Nicholas's or his father's? As she had thought before, her aunt had to be demented to think either of the Millward men would risk all this by turning to petty theft.

Jeremy answered the door himself, at her first ring. From the size of the house, she'd half expected a servant to answer.

'Caitlin, at last,' he exclaimed. 'I'd begun to think you weren't coming.'

'I'm sorry. Am I late? I walked, it was such a lovely evening. I also have to admit to being just a little nervous about coming,' she admitted laughingly.

'Oh, for heaven's sake, why?' Jeremy began. 'We're all friends here.'

'Well, walking alone into a roomful of strangers has never been my favourite occupation, and then, when I saw the house, suffice it to say, I've never been in anything halfway so magnificent.'

Jeremy laughed at her frankness. 'Oh, this old heap. It's been in the family for generations, handed down from father to son. I could never have afforded anything so grand. As it is, it's more than half shut up. Since my wife died three years ago, I've had no need of such a large place and Nicholas has his own house.'

Caitlin was puzzled. Surely Nicholas, being as wealthy as he must be, would help his father out with the costs of a house that would one day be his. But it was as if Jeremy had read her thoughts.

'Nicholas would pay the bills happily but I refuse to let him. It'll be his burden soon enough. And,' he added, leaning towards her conspiratorially, 'I like my independence.'

The pride of the man shone through the simple words but it was obvious to Caitlin that Jeremy Millward, at least, was far from being the rich man that the huge house suggested, which, not unnaturally, led her to assume that he couldn't afford to have the Pimpernel Gallery go out of business.

'Now, come, I'll introduce you to everyone. They're all eagerly awaiting.'

The warmth of his gaze told her he was perfectly genuine in his delight at having her as his guest. The voices, which had been loud, had ground to a halt and every eye turned towards the doorway as they entered the lounge.

'Here we are everyone. I want you to say hello to Caitlin. She's Jessica's niece, come to look after the Orion Gallery while poor Jessica is in hospital.'

At once, the various people who had been standing around in small groups, each with a glass and a plate in their hands, surrounded Caitlin and Jeremy. It was because of this that Caitlin failed to see the startled look that the tall, dark-haired man standing by the open french window directed at her, or hear the subdued murmur of the blonde at his side as she asked, 'Do you know her, Nicholas?'

'You could say that,' the man responded quietly.

'Nicholas,' Jeremy called. 'Come over here and meet Caitlin, and bring Amanda with you.'

Caitlin found herself face to face with the man she had so fervently hoped wouldn't be present. Just as she'd feared, Nicholas was finally approaching her. He took his time, it was true, and his features had lost their expression of contempt but, for all that, she was positive that he was every bit as displeased to see her as she was to see him.

It didn't help that the look in his eyes remained unfathomable. She should have grown accustomed to not being able to work out precisely what Nicholas Millward was thinking by this time. Yet, it never failed to irritate and exasperate her.

Just for once, she reasoned, why didn't he simply come out with whatever it was he was thinking? As usual, he frustrated that wish.

'Hello, Caitlin,' he murmured. 'I didn't expect to bump into you, and in my father's house of all places.'

3

In the name of good manners, Caitlin could do nothing else but take the hand that Nicholas was proffering. Thankfully, she saw that her fingers were perfectly steady, although her fleeting glance up at him, she guessed, betrayed the conflict of emotion that was battling on beneath.

Nicholas raised one eyebrow in the manner that she recalled so vividly from their previous encounters when something or someone had annoyed him. The only difference between then and now was the glint of amusement that accompanied it.

He had discerned her unease. She might have known he would. He'd proved himself only too astute in their various business dealings. Why should things be any different in their social encounters?

Caitlin stiffened. Despite her initial alarm upon seeing him across the room, she wasn't going to allow him to intimidate her. They weren't at work now. She was on holiday and as such, a free spirit. She could do as she pleased. The thought was intensely gratifying, but even so, she couldn't quite suppress her fears.

'How nice to see you again, Nicholas.'

Surprisingly, her voice sounded perfectly steady, although she was acutely aware of Jeremy's start of surprise at her side. He, of course, would have no notion that his son and Caitlin were already acquainted.

'Liar,' Nicholas murmured.

The single word was clearly meant for her ears alone. To anyone watching, his lips would hardly have moved. Stung by his manner and the mocking, little word, Caitlin pulled her hand abruptly from his.

'I'm surprised to see you here,' he went on, patently unperturbed by her

42

baleful glare. 'I thought you'd be at Gallagher's side, celebrating his victory in finally obtaining his asking price.'

'I'm on holiday.'

'Really.'

How was it, Caitlin wondered, that he could manage to make one small word sound so insulting.

'This is the first I've heard of it. Strange sort of holiday, isn't it? Manning a shop? I'd have thought you'd be better employed getting ready for when I arrive and take you over.'

Caitlin's long lashes fluttered. She blinked unsurely at him.

'Take me over? Don't you mean take Gallagher's over?'

'No, I mean take you over.'

For the first time, Caitlin saw concrete evidence of a sense of humour within Nicholas as his mouth twitched and his eyes gleamed. In that second, they lost their coolness. Minute, golden flecks appeared within their depths, lightening and warming them. It was an intriguing transformation and one that

Caitlin hadn't anticipated.

'Didn't Gallagher tell you before you left? I asked him to,' Nicholas drawled. 'I'd like you to be my personal assistant, Caitlin. Gallagher doesn't really need one any longer. You'd be answering solely to me, naturally. I was intending to see you and make the offer, officially, this week sometime.'

The slow, drawn-out smile that accompanied his words was little short of lethal. Caitlin's normally generous mouth tightened as she continued to stare at him. He couldn't be serious. Work with him? She'd as soon work with a cobra! Amusement glinted at her expression of horror.

'As I'm sure you appreciate, I'd like to know when you'll be back at work,' he finished.

Caitlin was sorely tempted to retort, never. She hadn't envisaged Nicholas himself coming in to run things. She'd heard he normally put his own people in to get things working as he wanted them, not that he himself employed a hands-on approach. Why should Gallagher's be different?

Caitlin took a deep breath and said, 'I'll be back at work in a month's time. Doctor's orders. I haven't been well.'

'What's wrong?' he demanded. 'You look all right to me.'

'Overwork and exhaustion.'

'I see.'

He was studying her. Caitlin lifted her chin, meeting his gaze courageously. It was a heady experience, she had to admit. Nonetheless, he wasn't going to be allowed to scare her. Nicholas Millward was going to be shown, in no uncertain manner, that it would take a better man than he was to daunt her. The trouble was, he remained sublimely unaware of what she was trying to do.

His tone was one of confident unconcern as he asked, her, 'Demanded too much, did I? If that's the case, you'd better let me know now. I demand total commitment from the people I employ.'

45

Caitlin bit down upon the words that flew to her tongue. She wasn't about to give him the satisfaction of slapping her down, in public, for insolence.

Instead, she said, 'I assure you that that's what you'll get, Mr Millward.'

'What happened to Nicholas?'

Caitlin managed a cool smile.

'Mr Millward seems more respectful, don't you think?'

She saw his lips tighten in annoyance with her and she only just prevented herself from laughing out loud.

'Oh, Nicholas will do, Caitlin. I don't demand formality from my employees.'

'No,' she murmured with a second, even sweeter smile, 'just total commitment.'

He must have decided to disregard her sarcasm although he did manage to disconcert her again with a long, considering look.

'You do look rather pale, I suppose. I'm just surprised that Gallagher didn't say something to me when I rang him earlier. Presumably he knows you're on extended leave?'

'Well, naturally he knows. He is — was,' she hastily amended, 'my boss. He gave me permission.'

'Yes, well, he should have consulted me first, given the present circumstances,' he drawled. 'Anyway, far be it from me to contradict medical opinion. Just make sure that you do rest and don't overdo things on your aunt's behalf. I don't want a wilting flower on my hands. There'll be a great deal to do to get things running to the standards I demand.'

The man was a sadist, Caitlin concluded sourly. She could see that she'd be looking for another job.

'Anyway, I'm sure we'll be seeing a lot of each other while you're here, so I can keep a watchful eye upon you, can't I?'

It was at this point that Jeremy must have decided to tactfully remind them of his own presence.

'I didn't realise you two knew each other. You didn't mention it, Nicholas.'

'I'm afraid I didn't make the connection, Father. You didn't mention Caitlin by name, did you? You just said you'd invited the latest resident of Chegston.'

'Aren't you going to introduce me, Nicholas?'

The second interruption came from Nicholas's companion and it was nowhere near as polite as Jeremy's had been. This was one facet of his reputation, at least, that he was living up to, Caitlin saw — the expected and, more or less obligatory, beautiful woman by his side.

She recalled the gossip that had abounded about him at Gallagher's when it was first learned who it was who was negotiating to buy them out. The office girls had practically fallen over themselves trying to attract his attention.

His open arrogance had irritated Caitlin at the time. It irritated her even more now. Just who did he think he was? Silly question, she decided. He was her boss, for the moment at any rate, and, as such, clearly determined to extract the most possible from the position. Even on a social level!

'Sorry, Amanda,' she heard Nicholas apologise. 'Meet Caitlin Mortimer. We're going to be working together. Caitlin is to be my new personal assistant.'

Caitlin gave him a sideways glance. He was clearly taking her acceptance of his job offer for granted. Now why should that surprise her, she mused, not without a good deal of irony.

However, if the news of her new position at Gallagher's had horrified Caitlin, it positively stunned Amanda. She clearly wasn't at all pleased, although she did force herself to utter a stilted little, 'Pleased to meet you, Caitlin.'

Despite Caitlin's low opinion of her new employer, as the other woman's slightly vacant blue eyes met her and the full red lips took on a petulant droop, she found herself wondering

49

what on earth a man like Nicholas Millward was doing with someone like this?

Gossip had connected him with several, high-society women, one or two of them married, but they had all been intelligent, well-respected women, as well as beautiful. That, of course, went without saying.

Amanda now took hold of Nicholas's arm, pressing herself against his side, simpering at him. Caitlin sniffed softly, and couldn't help a swift, sideways glance at Nicholas. A knowing smile told her that he was well aware of the way her thoughts were working. Her lips tightened as she turned back to Jeremy.

'Come along, Caitlin, my dear,' the older man said. 'Let's get you a drink and something to eat.'

Thankful to escape the appraising gaze of her new employer, Caitlin went with Jeremy. Much to her relief, the rest of the evening passed relatively uneventfully. The majority of Jeremy's guests proved charming people, more than ready to welcome an attractive stranger into their midst. Even Nicholas managed to hide any chagrin he might be experiencing at the presence of his future assistant.

The only person who continued to resent Caitlin's presence was Amanda, and Caitlin suspected that that was because she was being viewed as competition for Nicholas's attention. Well, Amanda needn't worry about that.

However, as the evening progressed, Caitlin began to entertain the faintest suspicion that Amanda might have just cause for her resentment and jealousy, because whenever Caitlin happened to glance Nicholas's way, it was to discover Nicholas's gaze fixed upon her. Whether this was because he was annoyed that she was here or because he found her attractive, she couldn't have said. The expression in those grey eyes told her nothing.

The other guests were all taking their

leave before he finally approached her again.

'How are you getting home, Caitlin? Did you come by car or did you walk?' he asked.

'I walked,' Caitlin replied. 'I'll do the same on my return. It's not far.'

'I have to run Amanda home. I'll drop you off as well.'

'There's really no need. I'm looking forward to the walk in the moonlight. It's a lovely night.'

'I think there is a need, Caitlin,' he contradicted quietly. 'No woman is safe at night, alone and on foot, not even in a village like Chegston. I'll run you home.'

Caitlin gave him no further argument. Nicholas wasn't making a request — he was issuing a command!

Caitlin did wonder fleetingly if Amanda would happily accept her company in the car with them with equal complacency. Something told her she wouldn't.

A bright voice interrupted her thoughts.

'I'm ready, Nicholas, darling. Oh, Caitlin.'

It was Amanda, and just as Caitlin had expected she would be, she looked distinctly dismayed to see Caitlin standing there.

'It was nice meeting you,' Amanda began, when Nicholas cut in with a curt, 'We're taking Caitlin with us, Amanda.'

Amanda's mouth dropped open and her eyes flew to Nicholas.

'But, surely, she only lives down the lane. Can't she walk if she hasn't got a car?'

The tone was that of a sulky child deprived of a promised treat. Caitlin had to turn away quickly before her broad smile gave her amusement away. Even so, as quick as she was, she knew that Nicholas had seen the beginnings of her laughter.

'There is no lighting at all in the lane, Amanda, and I'm not happy about her walking that far alone.'

The ill-matched trio made their way

outside in silence, where Caitlin made one final bid for independence.

'Look, I really could walk. The moonlight is so bright.'

Nicholas didn't bother to argue. He strode to his black saloon and flung the doors wide.

'Get in.'

Caitlin stalked towards the car, contenting herself with a baleful glare in Nicholas's direction instead of the words she wanted to fling at him. He met her look with silence as she took her seat in the rear of the vehicle.

She rather thought Nicholas had meant her to get into the front, beside him, but she had no intention of upstaging Amanda any more than she had to. It was bad enough that Nicholas was showing a callous disregard for his companion of the evening without Caitlin having the impertinence to do the same.

With no further ado, Nicholas slammed both doors shut and climbed into the driver's seat. He started up the powerful engine and with a deep-throated roar, the car took off down the lengthy driveway.

Outside the gates, he turned right instead of left as she had expected and she had her mouth open to say that the Orion Gallery was in the opposite direction when Amanda pre-empted her by saying, 'Surely we can take Caitlin home first. I was expecting you to come in, Nicholas, for a nightcap.'

'It's quicker to do it this way, Amanda. I can drop Caitlin off then on my way back home.'

Caitlin felt a surge of sympathy for Amanda. She looked rebuffed and dejected. This was all her fault. If she'd brought her car, then no-one would have felt obliged to give her a lift.

Nicholas's car came to a halt before a detached house set well back from the road, in extensive gardens. Nicholas immediately climbed out and walked round to open the front, passenger door. Amanda climbed out reluctantly.

Her lovely face was still set in sulky lines.

Nicholas didn't seem to notice. He took hold of her arm and walked along the unlit driveway. Tall bushes screened them from view as they got nearer the house so it was impossible for Caitlin to tell whether or not, once they reached the front door, Nicholas kissed her good-night. If he did, it couldn't have been much of a kiss because he was back almost immediately, lowering himself into the driver's seat.

'Come into the front, Caitlin.'

Caitlin stiffened. 'I'm fine where I am, thank you.'

Nicholas turned in his seat, his eyes shooting steel darts at her through the darkness.

'Frightened of me?'

Well, of course, just as she imagined he knew it would, that did it. He wasn't going to be able to accuse her of cowardice as far as he was concerned. Caitlin got out of the back and obediently positioned herself in the front.

'That's better,' Nicholas murmured. 'Now I can see you.'

'You've been able to see me all evening,' Caitlin retaliated, not even turning to face him as she spoke.

'True,' Nicholas conceded, 'but not like this.'

His eyes reflected the moonlight all of a sudden, gleaming silver, leaving Caitlin in no doubt as to his meaning. He meant that they were alone, in the close proximity of the car, with just the stars for company.

All the ingredients for a love scene, he probably imagined only, in the case of herself and Nicholas, such an outcome was most unlikely. Yet Nicholas was interested in her, there was no question about that. The real question, as far as Caitlin was concerned, was what particular form that interest took. Was it personal or, as seemed much more likely, was it one of business? Had he a card hidden up his sleeve still, one he hadn't deemed fit to play?

She still felt, as she had all along, that

for a man such as he, Nicholas had ceded victory far too readily over Patrick's asking price for the company. Caitlin hadn't trusted him then, and she didn't trust him now.

His gaze was contemplative as it met hers, intensifying her unease. He started up the engine of the car and it pulled away from the gateway, smoothly, silently.

Nicholas's profile was granite-like. The strong lines of jaw and throat seemed to be chiselled from stone. He lifted a long-fingered hand from the steering-wheel to flick a wayward strand of hair from his forehead. Caitlin felt something clench in her stomach. As much as she disliked him and his way of doing things, she had to admit that Nicholas Millward was a strikingly handsome man.

She smiled grimly to herself. If she agreed to become his personal assistant, she was going to have to work, no matter how briefly, with the man and, as such, any attraction that she might feel for him would make life extremely difficult. She sighed. Perhaps the best course of action all round would be for her to find herself another job.

She was reluctant to do that, though. She'd been at Gallagher's ever since she'd left school, conscientiously working her way up from typist to the position of Patrick's personal assistant. The most sensible course of action would be to wait and see how things worked out between herself and Nicholas. She sighed as she made a show of concentrating on the passing hedgerow.

'Why the sigh?' he asked.

Caitlin stiffened. As she'd already deduced on more than one occasion, Nicholas was too perceptive by half.

'No reason,' she replied.

'I hope that we will be able to work together satisfactorily,' he said unexpectedly. 'Rather more so than we've managed so far.'

So, he had perceived her hostility towards him. Strictly speaking, she wasn't really surprised, even though she'd struggled long and hard to hide it. Clearly, she needn't have bothered. He'd known all along.

'I hope so, too, Mr Millward.'

'Nicholas, Caitlin. My name is Nicholas. I thought we'd already established that. You and I are going to be spending a lot of time together from now on. If we can't maintain a good, working relationship, we may as well call it a day right now. So, what's it to be? Do we make a fresh start or do we call it quits here and now?'

It was perfectly clear to Caitlin that he meant every word he was saying. And she knew, in that second, that she didn't want to give up an ideal job with a company and a workforce that she respected and cared about. And when all was said and done, why should she?

'I enjoy my job, I always have, and I have to admit that I would be loath to give it up. I'm sure that for the short time that we'll be working together . . .'

'What do you mean? The short time?'

His tone was sharp.

'Well, surely, once you've got Gallagher's back on to its feet, you'll move on to something else? You always have before.'

'Caitlin, haven't I made myself clear?'

He appeared amused about something. Caitlin was puzzled.

'I thought you had.'

'You are to be my personal assistant, and that means what it says. You will assist me, wherever I happen to be working, not just at Gallagher's. Wherever I go, you would go,' he elaborated slowly.

'What!' Caitlin must have sounded every bit as horrified as she felt. 'But you must already have an assistant for that.'

'My dear girl, of course I had a personal assistant but I've promoted him, to clear room for you.' He smiled grimly.

'But you didn't mention that. I wouldn't have . . . '

'You wouldn't have accepted the

offer? Is that what you're trying to tell me?'

'I wasn't aware that I had officially accepted your offer as yet.'

'No, that's right, you haven't, have you? Not in actual words, at least.' Nicholas's voice was drily matter-of-fact. 'I had assumed that Gallagher had told you and, as I hadn't received your resignation, I thought it was all cut and dried. My mistake, obviously.'

Caitlin needed time to rethink. She hadn't realised the full implications of the position. She tried to stall for time.

'What will the job entail?'

'Why, as I've already said, you'll be at my side, working closely with me on all aspects of my business concerns. Don't you think you're up to the task?'

'Of course, I'm up to it,' she bit back. 'It's whether or not I wish to work that closely with you.'

'I see.'

Nicholas pulled the car to a standstill.

'In that case, we'd better have this

out right now, because if you aren't prepared to work with me, I'll have to find someone who is, and fast.' He ground the words out. 'What's your objection to working with me, Caitlin?'

'I hardly know you,' she blurted out.

'Don't be ridiculous. I'm offering you a job, not marriage. Why do you feel compelled to know me first? Did you know Patrick when you first worked with him?'

'No.'

'So, what's your objection?'

Caitlin couldn't answer him.

'Is it me?' he demanded impatiently. 'Do I repel you in some way?'

'No,' she burst out, 'of course you don't. Well, at least, not . . . '

'Well, come on, out with it. What is it?'

'I don't much care for some of your methods of working. I don't like your utter ruthlessness, the way you have of simply riding rough-shod over people. They don't seem to matter to you.'

Nicholas didn't say anything for a

long moment. His fingers began to tap out a beat upon the steering-wheel. It was a strangely disconcerting sound.

'Is that it? Is that your sole objection to working with me?'

Caitlin nodded, feeling extremely silly.

'Let me explain something to you, Caitlin. Sometimes, I have to be ruthless, as you phrase it. But, believe me, I never deliberately set out to hurt anyone, not if I can take steps to avoid it. How many people have I made redundant at Gallagher's?'

'None,' Caitlin mumbled.

'Precisely. It pays me to get the work force on my side and that's what I try to do. There were, and I'm erring on the conservative side now, around half a dozen people who, if I were as ruthless as you say I am, I would have had no compunction in getting rid of, one way or another, but for various reasons, I decided to keep them on. Most of them are near retirement. It's called natural wastage. Hardly the actions of a hatchet man.' His tone, as well as his smile, was dry now.

'But what about the way you backed Patrick into a corner, not once but several times. You made no effort to spare his feelings.'

'Caitlin,' Nicholas said as he strove for patience, 'I am, first and foremost, a business man. I will always try to get the best deal I can. I gave in in the end, didn't I? Patrick didn't lose out.'

'He would have, though, if you'd got your way.'

'But he didn't, did he? It's all part and parcel of the game. You'll have to understand that if you're to work with me. So, what do you say? Shall we give it a go? A trial period if you want. I can't be more flexible than that,' he concluded.

'OK.' Caitlin heard herself agree grudgingly. 'A trial period. And then I'll reassess the situation. Six months?' she suggested.

'Should be long enough,' Nicholas agreed.

Nicholas restarted the car and slid it into gear.

'Well, now that that's out of the way, there was something else I wanted to discuss.'

Caitlin's mouth tightened. He looked like the cat that had just managed to sip the cream. She drew a deep breath. He'd been sure of her agreement all the way along.

'Really?' she said tightly. 'And what would that be?'

'The little matter of the thefts from the Orion. Your aunt has told you about them, presumably?'

'Naturally,' Caitlin replied.

He glanced at her. 'Are you staying there alone?'

'Yes.'

'I thought she had a son. Why hasn't he been dragooned into service? Surely he's more fitted to the task than you.'

'Jessica didn't consider him so. He is only just twenty.'

'To my knowledge, you've had no experience of art galleries and I certainly don't see you in the role of shopkeeper.'

'Perhaps you don't, but it really isn't anything to do with you, is it?'

'It is when the person who is undertaking the job of guarding threatened works of art is the person whom I have earmarked to be my closest helpmate.'

Why did he have to make it sound as if they were about to become the most intimate of associates? It made her feel uneasy, mainly because she couldn't imagine Nicholas becoming mildly friendly, let alone intimate, with anyone who worked for him.

'What will you do if a painting goes missing while you're in charge?'

'What my aunt did — report it to the police. What else?'

'You know my father made her an offer for the place a couple of years ago?'

'Yes, and she turned it down. It was after that that the thefts began.'

That was a mistake. She knew it the

second the words had left her tongue. It sounded as if she were accusing his father. She chewed on her bottom lip, waiting for the explosion. It wasn't quite an explosion that followed but Nicholas did turn and look at her very sharply.

'I trust that that doesn't mean what it sounds like?'

'No. I didn't really mean anything.'

'You didn't?'

'I was simply stating the facts as they took place. The first robbery, according to Aunt Jessica, took place six weeks afterwards.'

But Nicholas wasn't to be pacified. He'd instinctively picked up the intonation in her voice. Caitlin could have kicked herself. She could have landed both her aunt and herself in hot water with her careless remark. And it wasn't as if she even believed that Jeremy had had anything to do with the thefts. Nicholas's face darkened in a frown.

'What do you know of the relationship between my father and your aunt?'

'That they're business rivals, obviously. That they have known each other a long time . . . '

'Is that all you know?' His voice still had an edge to it.

'Yes.'

'What has she said to you about him with regards to her conviction that he's out to get the gallery off her, by one means or another?'

Caitlin was at a loss for words. It was obvious from Nicholas's questions that the Millwards had heard rumours of Jessica's suspicions as to who was doing the stealing. Her own words would surely only have fuelled those rumours. She could kick herself.

'So, she has said something.' Nicholas's expression was grim by this time. 'You'd better warn your aunt that if I hear any more people repeating the things she's been saying, or rather, insinuating, I'll be talking to my solicitor. So far, my father hasn't heard the talk. I want to keep it that way. Is that clear, Caitlin?'

Caitlin felt numb. She couldn't have spoken then if her very life had depended upon it.

'She'd also be well advised, after her recent heart attack, to consider my father's extremely generous offer rather more seriously. She's going to be in no fit state to run a gallery for quite some time to come.'

'I'm here.'

'Not for long, Caitlin. Believe me, not for long. I want you where you belong, at Gallagher's and at my side. You tell her what I've said.'

'Are you threatening her?' Caitlin demanded, furious now.

'No, merely advising, as I have just pointed out. If it had been anyone other than my father, she'd have taken the offer. I suspect it's all been getting a bit too much for Jessica of late. She's not getting any younger after all.'

'And neither is your father,' Caitlin retaliated smartly.

'Quite,' Nicholas put in blandly, 'but my father's got me to help him when necessary. Who has your aunt got? David? I think not.'

'How dare you? And what do you mean, if it had been anyone else but your father?'

'Why don't you ask Jessica that question?' he put in smoothly. 'Or maybe you already know the answer, but you're just not saying.'

'I don't know what you're talking about. Despite what you think, Jessica really doesn't want to sell, not to your father, not to anyone.'

By this time, they'd reached the Orion Gallery and Nicholas pulled the car to a halt.

'My father is a remarkably patient man, Caitlin, but even his patience will eventually run out. I just can't see why it's Jessica that has this grudge. It really ought to be the other way round.'

'But, surely . . . ' Caitlin was puzzled by what he said. She frowned at him. 'Isn't it your father who bears the grudge? That's what Jessica believes.'

'You really don't know what's behind

your aunt's hostility, do you?'

'What should I know? You keep hinting at something. Why don't you just say what it is? All I know is that Jessica beat your father to the purchase of the Orion Gallery and he's resented it ever since.'

'So that's Jessica's story, is it?' His tone was one of extreme irony.

'Yes. I wish you'd stop talking in riddles, Nicholas. I've had a long day. I want to go in and go to bed. If you know any other reason for all of this, then I wish you'd tell me and have done with it.'

'It's not my place to tell you, Caitlin, if as you say, you really don't know. It's between your aunt and my father.'

Caitlin got out of the car. Nicholas leaned across the seat where she had just been sitting and stopped her from closing the door.

'Be careful, Caitlin, while you're here alone. That last robbery, the one where they drove a car through the window, was a nasty one. It means they'll stop at nothing to get what they want. And I'd really like my assistant to turn up for work in one piece.'

Caitlin slammed the door, almost in his face. He didn't really care about her well-being. He was simply concerned with the future well-being of Gallagher's. She glared at him as he slipped the car into gear but then made no move to go. He was evidently waiting to see her inside. Caitlin turned and, in some relief that the evening was over, unlocked the door and went in.

4

As she walked up the stairs to the flat, puzzling over the things that Nicholas had said, Caitlin heard the phone ringing. It was the hospital. Jessica had had another attack! A much more serious one this time. Could she find David and get to the hospital immediately?

Caitlin hadn't the foggiest idea of David's present whereabouts. Jessica's address book was no help and, deciding that even if she couldn't locate David, she herself could be at her aunt's side, she ran out to her car and drove straight to the hospital.

'It's all right, Miss Mortimer, your aunt's out of immediate danger, for the moment,' the night sister told Caitlin once she had explained that she had been unable to find David.

'Can I see her?'

'Well,' the sister said doubtfully, 'just for a moment or two. She's sleeping. We're keeping her sedated, for her own good. She's a very ill woman, Miss Mortimer. She's been under stress for too long.'

Caitlin looked down at her aunt and felt the sting of tears in her eyes. She looked so small, so vulnerable, so pale. What had happened to the feisty woman with the astringent tongue?

Why hadn't she told the family that she was labouring under such stress? It must be the worry of the thefts. It couldn't be anything else. The thief had to be caught. Caitlin was suddenly determined about that. She'd go to the police station in the morning and begin to put some pressure on them to find whoever was responsible.

In the worry of the moment, Caitlin forgot the questions she had wanted to ask her aunt, the questions that Nicholas's strange remarks had raised. They could wait. The main thing now was for her aunt to recover. That was all that mattered.

The next morning, Caitlin left the gallery closed and went along to the local police station. She asked to see whoever was in charge of the investigation into the gallery thefts. She was duly shown into the office of a Sergeant Wilmot.

'I'm very sorry to hear about your aunt, Miss Mortimer,' he said, once Caitlin had told him of her reasons for being there, 'but we had very little to go on at the time. There were no finger prints, other than those of your aunt and her son, and of course, of the various customers of the gallery. It's an impossible task really. Too many people coming and going. And the first two do seem to be simple cases of shop-lifting. It was the last one that was the most worrying.'

'You mean the car being driven through the window?'

'Yes. The car had been stolen, of course, and then later abandoned. They'd even wiped that clean of any prints. We traced it back to its owner. Up till that time, I must admit, we did wonder if it was an inside job. It could still have been, and just done that way to make it look like an outside job.'

'An inside job? But that would mean either my aunt or David? That's ridiculous, sergeant.'

'I don't know if you're aware of it, Miss Mortimer, but your aunt did employ various assistants from time to time and we did wonder if one of them could be responsible. However, they all proved to be in the clear. Another difficulty, of course, was that no-one could pinpoint the exact time that the paintings were taken.'

He shrugged his broad shoulders.

'And, although valuable, they were both fairly small, easy to slip under a coat, or into a shopping bag,' he continued. 'The final incident, the one with the stolen car, had been planned. I would say it wasn't the same person responsible for all three thefts and in such a case, it's very difficult to catch the culprits. The paintings, as yet, haven't been found. So someone's keeping them well hidden, or they might have been smuggled abroad and into a private collection of some sort.'

And that was that. There was no further help to be had there at the moment.

But it wasn't the end of Caitlin's problems, not by any means. The following day, David turned up at the shop, accompanied by a weird-looking girl whom he introduced as Donna, his girlfriend.

'Oh, David, I'm so glad to see you. Your mother's had another heart attack,' Caitlin said immediately.

'OK now, is she?' David asked.

'She's still very weak, and she's been asking for you. I tried your flat yesterday.' Jessica had recovered enough to give Caitlin Donna's address. 'But you weren't there.'

'Well, you'll know where I am from now on. Donna and I will be staying here for a week or two. Just till we find somewhere else to live.'

'Somewhere else? What do you mean?'

'Haven't been able to keep up with the rent. They've turned us out.'

'Oh.' Caitlin regarded the two of them dubiously. 'Have you cleared that with your mother?'

She couldn't imagine her fastidious aunt being pleased to have Donna living in her flat. She was really aggressive-looking and didn't show any interest in Jessica's welfare. Caitlin couldn't take to her at all.

David had clearly come under her influence, dressed completely in black, dirty-looking clothes, and his normally wavy hair was cropped really short. Caitlin hadn't recalled him being quite this way-out the last time she'd seen him. She wondered if Donna were the bad influence. It was no wonder Jessica hadn't wanted him in charge of her precious gallery.

'Oh, Mum won't mind. I'll go and see her later, and tell her. We've done it before. Donna was thrown out of her last place, too.'

'I see. Well, there are three bedrooms and I don't suppose your mother will be home just yet.'

'Donna and I share.'

'Of course, silly of me.' Caitlin felt foolish, and quickly changed the subject.

'If you could just stay put in the shop for a while, David, I'll just slip out and pick up a few extra things, food and suchlike.'

'Sure.'

Caitlin picked up her handbag and left the gallery, still very much preoccupied with what seemed a series of mounting problems. In fact, she was so preoccupied that, but for a man's hand reaching out and yanking her back on to the pavement, she might have ended up under the wheels of a passing truck.

'Life proving too much of a strain for you?' Nicholas's biting tones demanded. 'What on earth did you think you were doing? But for me, you could have been killed, or at the very least, ended up in a bed alongside your aunt.'

Caitlin put a shaking hand to his and pushed it off her arm.

'I'm fine now, thank you.'

'Oh, I am glad. Please don't feel under any obligation to thank me for my timely intervention.'

Caitlin dashed a still shaking hand across her eyes.

'I'm sorry. Thank you, Nicholas. That was unforgiveable of me. I've got rather a lot on my mind, as you probably guessed.'

'Yes.' He paused before going on to say, 'I was sorry to hear of Jessica's second attack. We both were, my father and I. How is she?'

Caitlin raised her chin to look up at him, her eyes sparkling defiantly in the light of what she deemed a totally insincere remark. How was she ever going to work with him? Perhaps she would just resign, here and now, but, somehow, the words just wouldn't present themselves. Instead, she heard herself saying, 'Not very well, Nicholas, if you really want to know.'

'Of course, I want to know. Why else would I have asked?'

'How about as one way of finding out if my return to Gallagher's will be delayed?'

'Caitlin,' Nicholas said slowly and with a marked show of patience, 'whatever I may have said about your aunt, I wouldn't wish her ill. Please, believe that.'

'Why should I?' she went on. 'After all, her death would allow your father and you to have your way and buy the gallery.'

She heard Nicholas's indrawn breath and caught the flash of steel within the grey eyes. He did seem to bring out the very worst in her. At this rate, she wouldn't need to resign. He'd most probably sack her!

'I'm sorry,' she began to apologise.

'I'll forget you said that, Caitlin.' He spoke calmly and quietly. It didn't make the subsequent threat sound any less potent. 'But I'll warn you, my girl, you're going to have to curb that tongue of yours or you and I are going to spend our next six months together fighting. And, whatever you might think to the contrary, that's the last thing that I want.'

And with that, he turned and walked away, leaving Caitlin gazing after him, open-mouthed.

★ ★ ★

A full week had gone by since Jessica's second heart attack and still Caitlin hadn't had a chance to ask her about Nicholas's remarks concerning her aunt and Jeremy.

In Caitlin's opinion, Jessica didn't seem to be making any headway at all, although the sister in charge of the ward expressed satisfaction with her progress.

Jessica did manage to express her relief to her niece, however, about the fact that David had moved back into the flat above the gallery.

For the first time, Caitlin wondered if her son's behaviour had contributed in any way to Jessica's illness. When Jessica made no mention of Donna, Caitlin decided to say nothing either.

The gallery had always closed on a Wednesday and Caitlin took advantage of that and the fact that it was a glorious, summer day to walk through the village and take a look at Pimpernel Gallery and Antiques. As luck would have it, both Jeremy and Nicholas were inside. Jeremy saw her at once and beckoned her in.

'Caitlin, how nice. To what do we owe this honour?'

He sounded genuinely pleased to see her.

'I was out for a walk and I thought . . . '

'And you thought you'd take a look at the competition.' Nicholas interrupted with characteristic bluntness. 'Come to see if we've any particularly interesting paintings in here? Is that it,

Caitlin? Well, feel free.' He indicated the room at large. 'Have a good look round. Actually, you've saved me a walk. I was coming along to see you at the Orion later.'

'Oh, really. What for?'

As angry as she was with him, she refused to descend to his level and accuse him of snooping. Nonetheless, her glance at him was decidedly sour.

'To discover the exact date you're due back at Gallagher's. It's all been left rather vague, in my opinion. And as, in the light of your absence, Gallagher's collapse seems imminent, according to your previous employer, I decided I needed to know.'

'Why didn't you simply ask my previous employer?' she demanded waspishly. 'He knows.'

'I'd rather ask you,' Nicholas murmured, provocatively, Caitlin decided.

'Caitlin, my dear, take no notice of my son. He's in a strange mood today.' Jeremy glanced warmly at Nicholas, who took absolutely no notice at all.

'Come here and sit down,' Jeremy went on, indicating a chair which she hadn't noticed before, placed as it was just behind an antique bookcase. 'You can share our afternoon tea. I've just made a pot and there are some delicious, home-made scones, although, I can't lay claim to having made those. My housekeeper, Mrs Dillon, obliged.'

'Oh, no, please. I don't want to disturb you.'

'You're not disturbing us, dear girl. Far from it. It's very quiet today. I haven't seen a soul. Nicholas will tell you, I practically fell upon him in my eagerness to converse with a fellow human being.'

Jeremy had a dry, acerbic wit and it induced a warm smile from Caitlin now.

'How is Jessica?' Nicholas asked surprisingly. 'Any signs of her being discharged yet?'

Caitlin eyed him in a somewhat jaundiced manner. Still running true to form, evidently, despite the teasing manner of a moment ago. Well, she refused to be bullied into a premature return to work.

In a tone that all too accurately reflected her emotions, she told him, 'Not yet, Nicholas,' and just so that her position would be transparently clear to him added, 'In any case, whether my aunt is discharged or not, I shall remain here until the end of my month's holiday, August the twenty-sixth, as you're so desperate to know. Doctor's orders.'

'Oh, Caitlin, forgive me,' Jeremy put in before Nicholas could respond to this, 'I should have asked you straight away how your aunt is. I was so distressed to hear of her second attack.'

And, in stark contrast to his heartless son, he really did seem so.

Caitlin had to admit that Jeremy didn't strike her as a man with a grudge against Jessica. Yet, it seemed that her aunt genuinely believed that he resented her enough to try to force her out of the Orion Gallery by whatever means he had at his disposal. It couldn't just be down to the rivalry between them over the ownership of the Orion. There had to be something else, as Nicholas had already implied. It seemed to be something back in their past. Nicholas knew what it was. If only he'd tell her.

'She's improving daily, so I'm told, although, I have to say, I can't see it. It'll be a long haul back in any case. And she mustn't have any strains imposed upon her. I can't see her being able to man the gallery for quite some time yet.'

'She'll have to employ someone then, to do it for her,' Nicholas put in abruptly.

'I'm sure she will,' Caitlin retaliated.

This was precisely what she had meant when she accused Nicholas of having a ruthless disregard for other people. Nonetheless, she knew it would be putting her job on the line to point that out. She let her expression do it for her as she glared at him.

Nicholas understood. However, it didn't stop him from adding, 'As long as you don't go getting any ridiculous ideas about stopping on here. I need you at Gallagher's. Is that understood, Caitlin? There are several queries that only you, apparently, can sort out.'

'But surely, Nicholas,' Jeremy protested, 'you could make an exception in this instance? You can see how Caitlin's placed. Isn't there anyone else who can help you out?'

'Father, I'd be obliged if you'd stay out of this. It's between Caitlin and me. If Jessica had sold out when you offered to buy, the chances are that she wouldn't be lying in hospital, the victim of two heart attacks.'

'Nicholas,' Jeremy began to protest, 'is that really necessary?'

'But the fact is she didn't sell out and she is lying in hospital,' Caitlin snapped. 'What am I supposed to do? Abandon her?'

'No.' Nicholas's tone was perfectly even, providing a stark contrast to

Caitlin's slightly hysterical one. 'In the absence of any staff, she does have a son. Let him take over. I need you back at Gallagher's at the end of the month, Caitlin, and I don't want to hear anything further on the subject. Is that clear?'

Caitlin's shoulders slumped. What was the use of arguing? She took the cup of tea from Jeremy without realising what she was doing.

'Why don't you and Nicholas go out together this evening?' It was Jeremy, tentatively trying to put things right between them. 'Sort out some kind of compromise.'

He looked angrily at his son. 'You don't want to start off on a bad footing, if you have to work together, do you? Could make things very difficult, for both of you.'

Nicholas remained silent as Jeremy went on.

'Besides which, I should imagine it would make a pleasant change for you to have an intelligent female to converse with, Nicholas, rather than the brainless sort you usually find yourself with.' Jeremy's eyes were now twinkling with fun. 'Not that I would go as far as to mention names, of course,' he concluded.

Caitlin choked back a giggle, making out that she'd swallowed a mouthful of tea the wrong way. Nicholas wasn't deceived for a second. He exacted instant revenge.

'Yes, why don't we?' he said, and his lips curved in a self-congratulatory smile as he saw the horror that dawned in Caitlin's eyes.

'Oh, really — no — um, I don't think so.' She stumbled lamely to a halt. 'I don't think it would be entirely appropriate, given our respective positions.'

'Oh, come now, Caitlin, you really can't refuse an order from your employer, can you?' His smile was one of subtle triumph. 'After all, if we're going to be working as closely together in the future, as I envisage, there are bound to be occasions when we will be forced to confront each other over the dinner table. Perhaps we should get in some practice.'

She was beaten. The only thing she could do was give in as gracefully as she could, even though her heart was hammering fit to burst. Then a little devil seemed to get into her. Trying to be clever, was he? Well, two could play at that game.

'But what will Amanda have to say about this so-called practice?'

She had the satisfaction then of knowing that she'd surprised him. Not for long, however. In the next instance, he'd made the perfect recovery.

'Amanda? What, pray, does Amanda have to do with me asking you out?'

His voice had sharpened as he asked the question because, of course, he knew exactly what Caitlin was implying. He wasn't about to put it into words, though. He was going to quite calmly wait for Caitlin to do that for him.

'Well, you were with her on the night of your father's party. I rather assumed she must be your current girlfriend.'

'My girlfriend!' Nicholas exclaimed. 'God forbid! Although, I suspect she'd like to be.'

Caitlin almost snorted aloud, so great was her irritation with him. 'I see. Poor Amanda,' she said, maddened by his arrogance.

'There's no poor Amanda about it. She's well aware of the score, I can assure you of that,' Nicholas was saying.

'Come on, Caitlin,' Jeremy urged. 'Go out with him and let him experience the pleasure of an evening spent with a real woman. One who'll argue back,' and he winked at her.

To her utter astonishment, Caitlin found herself agreeing.

'OK, you're on,' she said. 'There's nothing I enjoy more than a good, spirited discussion.'

Nicholas gave a mock groan. 'What have I let myself in for?'

'Why,' she said and turned a perfectly

guileless gaze upon him, 'an evening of full and frank conversation. And I'm sure we've got lots to discuss.'

Not least, the question of whether she could stay on to mind the gallery for Jessica!

5

When they arrived at the restaurant two evenings later, Caitlin saw that there was a dance floor and a full orchestra, so it wouldn't be just a meal! That threw her. She didn't know how she'd cope with being held in Nicholas's arms if he wished to dance.

She directed a glance his way. Had he known there would be dancing? Knowing Nicholas as she was beginning to, she suspected that the temptation to wield his authority and place her in a difficult position would have proved too powerful for him to resist.

The worrying thing was that thoughts of him were beginning to occupy far too large a portion of her day, and her night. She glanced at him again as they followed the head waiter to their table. Nicholas looked so handsome — she couldn't deny that, which made Caitlin all the more thankful that she'd taken as much time and trouble over her own choice of outfit.

Caitlin had opted for black, silk evening trousers and an ivory, silk blouse. Her small waist was emphasised by a wide belt. She wondered if Nicholas had even noticed what she wore. Did he consider this merely a business meeting? Caitlin wouldn't be surprised if he hadn't come armed with a list of current problems at Gallagher's!

Once they were seated and the waiter had brought them their aperitifs, Nicholas raised his glass to her.

'Here's to your aunt, Caitlin, and her very speedy recovery,' he said.

At first, Caitlin made no response. She still couldn't rid herself of the notion that it wasn't only her aunt's health that concerned him but more the speed with which Caitlin could return to work.

'Thank you, Nicholas. I'll pass on your good wishes when I see her. I haven't had the opportunity yet to ask her about your remarks concerning your father and herself.'

'I wish you'd forget what I said, Caitlin. I spoke out of turn. I shouldn't have said anything. It's really none of my affair.'

'Oh, but it is. If you feel that my aunt is taking an unfair attitude towards your father, it's very much your affair. I just wish you'd tell me what you think, or, rather, know is behind it all.'

'Well, I'm not going to. It's between them.' He shrugged. 'If one of them decides to tell you, then all well and good. Now, forget them and choose what you want to eat. I see the waiter heading our way.'

What was there between Jessica and Nicholas's father? There was something, she was increasingly convinced. And it was more than her aunt was letting on, that was for sure. The moment Jessica was well enough, Caitlin intended asking her.

She studied the menu without

actually reading any of the words. It couldn't be anything too serious, surely? Jeremy seemed to feel no rancour towards her. It was Nicholas who exhibited all the ill-feeling.

'Madam?'

Caitlin looked up at the waiter and then quickly back at the menu. She selected the first dishes that her glance alighted upon.

'I'll have the melon and then the poached salmon in white wine, please.'

'Well, that certainly required a great deal of thought.' Nicholas sounded sarcastic. 'I don't think your mind is fully with me, is it, Caitlin? I'll have to see what I can do to change that. Dance?'

Without giving her time to refuse, he grasped her by the hand and pulled her to her feet.

Caitlin, knowing it would be useless to argue with him while he was in this mood, followed him on to the dance floor. Nicholas turned to face her and pulled her into his arms.

'What? No argument, Caitlin? That must be a first.'

Caitlin didn't speak. She couldn't have if she'd wanted to. She was far too aware of the physical strength of the man holding her in his arms. Throughout all of their dealings together, she'd never actually been this close to Nicholas Millward before, and she found it totally disconcerting.

A small flutter of excitement began to unfurl in the pit of her stomach, triggered, no doubt, by the sheer masculine appeal of this man. Caitlin stiffened, drawing back slightly, desperately seeking to put some distance between them. Nicholas tightened his hold.

Caitlin knew then that she had to behave normally, otherwise Nicholas was going to realise what was wrong. Her natural responses were humiliating enough as it was, without having him guess the effect he was having upon her. Frantically, she cast about for some suitable conversation. She took her cue from Nicholas's comment on her willingness to dance.

'Would it have done me any good to argue?'

'Not a bit,' Nicholas assured her. 'Just as it will do you no good to argue about staying on here to mind the gallery.'

He didn't look directly at her as he spoke but Caitlin had no trouble discerning the resolve that lay behind the innocent-sounding words. It was obvious that he had guessed her intention to try to persuade him to grant her indefinite time off and had already made his decision.

'But I can't simply leave. What will Jessica do? I do have some loyalty towards her, you know.'

'You also have a loyalty to Gallagher's, Caitlin, and you're the only one to have the complete picture of the last twelve months' trading at your fingertips. You know the customers and are used to dealing with them. Your experience will be invaluable to me over the first weeks and I intend to make full use of it. For that I need you there, on the spot.'

'Patrick will be there.'

'Do me a favour!' Nicholas snorted. 'He's about as much use as a sun hat in the rain. Why do you think he left so much of the work to you during our negotiations? He knew you were more on the ball than he is and to get the price he wanted, he had to prove the viability of the business. No, I need you there and you will be there, the second your month's up.'

The band had changed tempo from the waltz they had been playing to a more up-beat number. Caitlin decided it gave her a much-needed opportunity to free herself from Nicholas's firm grasp.

'Oh, no, you don't,' Nicholas murmured into her hair as she attempted to widen the gap between them. Indeed, he seemed to pull her even more closely to him. 'I've no time for this modern style of dancing. I like my women in my arms, right where they should be.'

'I'll bet you do,' Caitlin mumbled into his shoulder. 'And, just so that neither of us is under any illusion, I am not your woman.'

Nicholas made no response. However, she couldn't have missed his lightning grin. Maddeningly, Nicholas turned out to be a remarkably skilful dancer. Was there nothing he didn't do well? He moved her easily about the floor, whirling her round until she wasn't sure if it was his quickness of step that made her head spin or his sheer proximity.

All she knew was that by the time he guided her back to their table, she was gasping for breath.

'You're out of condition, Caitlin,' he murmured smoothly, his glance moving to her pink cheeks. 'I'll set you a course of exercises, if you like.'

His grin seemed wolfish all of a sudden and it was all that was needed to fuel Caitlin's suspicions of precisely what his intentions were.

'I don't think that will be necessary, Nicholas, thank you. Walking is my usual method of keeping fit.'

'Well, you don't do enough of it then, my girl.'

'I am not your girl and I didn't come out with you to be criticised for my lack of exercise.'

'Well, in that case, why don't you tell me just why you did come out with me, Caitlin?'

All traces of amusement had vanished. His eyes glinted tantalisingly as he watched her searching in vain for suitable words to answer him.

Fortunately, Caitlin was saved the trouble by the waiter setting her first course on the table before her. By the time he'd done that for both of them and had the bottle of wine uncorked, tasted and poured, Nicholas appeared to have forgotten what he'd asked. Caitlin didn't remind him.

The rest of the evening passed uneventfully with a mutually, if unspoken, agreement to a temporary lull in hostilities. Nicholas talked about his various activities, both business and leisure and, considerately for him, Caitlin decided sourly, displayed a keen interest in hers.

6

David and Donna had been living at the flat above the Orion Gallery for almost a fortnight when Caitlin, having seen or heard no evidence of the room they shared being tidied or cleaned, decided she'd better take a peek inside.

One look confirmed her fears and, as it was her free day, she decided to do the tidying for them. She'd already vacuumed and polished the rest of the apartment so she might as well finish with this room.

She'd made up the bed with clean sheets and pillowcases and had polished most of the furniture when she came to the dressing-table. It was chaotic. Bottles had been spilled, used tissues lay all over its surface, as if some attempt had been made to mop up the mess. Brushes and combs were strewn about, and Donna's make-up had stained the wood.

Jessica's lace mats were filthy and virtually ruined. Caitlin did the only thing she could. She began to remove everything, intending to wash the mats and then replace them. She was lifting object after object, placing them to one side on a nearby shelf, when a small packet, partially concealed beneath a large make-up pouch, caught her eye.

With a feeling of disquiet, she picked it up. It contained a quantity of fine, white powder. She couldn't be sure, but her first thought was that she had stumbled on drugs!

It must be Donna's. It had been concealed amongst her things. Caitlin frowned down at the small packet. What should she do? Had Donna persuaded David to try it? He must know it was here, unless Donna was concealing it from him? No wonder the girl hadn't been able to pay the rent on her flat. It was probably taking her all her time to come up with the money to feed her apparent addiction.

Caitlin considered the packet in her hand. She couldn't tell Jessica, that was for sure. Maybe she ought to speak to David. Almost at once, her instincts assured her that that would be futile. Suddenly, one name sprang to mind, as naturally as if it had every right to be there.

Nicholas! He could advise her on the best thing to do.

Caitlin swiftly replaced everything on the dressing-table. David and Donna would be out all day, as they were most days, so there would be no fear of Donna discovering the absence of the packet.

She'd go right now to the Pimpernel Gallery and, as she made up her mind, she hoped that Nicholas would be there. She slipped on a jacket.

She was halfway along the main street of the village before her steps began to falter. Supposing Nicholas decided that it was none of his business, that he didn't wish to become embroiled in her family's affairs? That was a more than strong possibility after the way in which he'd spoken about Jessica and her son.

Despite the fact that Nicholas's car was parked out front, it was Jeremy who appeared when the shop doorbell rang. Caitlin looked up and saw herself on a small television screen — closed circuit surveillance. It hadn't been there the last time she was in, she was sure.

A quick glance around showed her the camera, fixed unobtrusively at the back of the counter. This was what Jessica should instal. She'd have the thieves on film then. It could be the answer to all her problems. It would also remove her suspicions of Nicholas and his father once and for all.

'Caitlin!' Jeremy exclaimed. 'What a pleasure to see you. How are you? Nicholas has just been telling me all about your evening out.'

The cheeky grin on the older man's face told Caitlin precisely what he was implying, that Nicholas might have made advances to her!

But Nicholas, contrary to his father's expectations, had behaved with all the propriety of a Victorian gentleman.

When they'd finished their meal, he'd driven her back to the Orion, even walking to the side door that led up to the flat with her. However, upon reaching it, he had shaken her hand, which had somewhat disappointed Caitlin who had been looking forward to smartly putting him in his place if he made as much as a single move to kiss her.

Not knowing what else to do to cover her own feelings, Caitlin had wished him a cool good-night and closed the door.

As she had no intention of confiding any of this to Jeremy, it was quite a relief to hear Nicholas's voice.

'Well, Caitlin, checking up on the opposition again? You never give up, do you? I only hope you apply the same brand of dedication to your work with me.'

Caitlin swung round to face him.

'How are you, cat's eyes?' he said. 'I hadn't considered the matter before but your name is really most appropriate.'

'So I've been told, on more than one occasion,' Caitlin retorted.

'Oh, dear.' Nicholas sighed. 'And here I was, thinking I was being smart and terribly original.'

Caitlin ignored his teasing. She was becoming accustomed to his lightning mood changes, although how she'd get on working with them, she hadn't, as yet, allowed herself to consider.

'Could you spare me a few moments, Nicholas?' she went on to ask. 'Would you mind if I whisked him off for a while, Jeremy?'

'By all means, my dear. I'm not my son's keeper. I'm sure I'd have my work cut out if I was. Take him where you will, Caitlin. He's all yours.'

Nicholas's smile broadened then, at his father's lighthearted words.

'What more can I add, Caitlin?'

He flung his arms wide, as if he were about to take hold of her and draw her into his embrace. Caitlin took a hasty step backwards. She'd been held in his arms once and all it had done was point out to her her weakness of will as far as Nicholas was concerned.

'Where do you want to take me?' he teased. 'And, more to the point, what do you want me to do for you once there?'

The meaning in those last few provocative words couldn't be misunderstood. His grin now was wolfish. Caitlin felt herself blushing.

'I love a woman who blushes. So few do today.' Nicholas then murmured in an undertone, 'I'm going to enjoy working with you, Caitlin.'

The few, well-chosen words did what nothing else could have. So much so, that Caitlin wondered if he'd deliberately selected them, in an effort to remind her of who he was — her boss. The colour fled from her face leaving her almost ashen. Nicholas's glance at her then was sharp and full of concern.

'What's wrong, Caitlin?'

'Well.' She glanced uncomfortably at Jeremy.

Jeremy, proving himself to be every bit as perceptive as his son, said, 'Nicholas, she wants to speak to you alone. Take her upstairs. I'll be busy down here till lunchtime. You won't be interrupted.'

'Right. Follow me, Caitlin,' Nicholas said, taking command with assurance as he took hold of her arm. His gaze was still fixed upon her anxious, pale face.

Nicholas turned to face Caitlin once he'd guided her into the upstairs room that was obviously Jeremy's office. It was surprisingly spacious, allowing plenty of room for the large, mahogany desk that sat plump in its centre. Filing cabinets lined one wall, while a floor-length window almost filled another.

Several rows of shelves on the third wall held what looked like an army of reference books, all, not unnaturally, appertaining to antiques and fine art. A three-seater settee faced the desk and it was towards this that Nicholas waved Caitlin. Caitlin shook her head at him. Under the circumstances, she preferred to stand.

Nicholas walked towards her. He lifted a hand and she felt his fingers upon her cheek. For a crazy, impulsive moment the temptation to nuzzle her face into his hand, as the cat that he had likened her to would have, was almost too powerful to withstand.

Somehow, she resisted the urge and took a step back for the second time. She couldn't think straight, let alone breathe, when he was that close. The realisation was a chastening one. Nicholas Millward was beginning to have a very powerful effect upon her.

Nicholas, interpreting her withdrawal as a sign of rejection, allowed his hand to drop to his side and Caitlin watched uneasily as his jaw hardened. He turned away from her, walking across to the window, thrusting the offending hand deep into his trouser pocket as he did so.

He stood looking down on to the street below and his voice was harsh as he asked, 'What was it you wanted to talk to me about?'

She shouldn't have come, Caitlin reflected unhappily. She'd given way to impulse and she should have known better. He wasn't interested in her and her problems.

'I'm sorry, Nicholas. I shouldn't have bothered you. I really shouldn't have come. I don't know what I was thinking of,' she muttered. 'I'll go. It's not your problem.'

She turned, preparing to leave the room. What she would say to Jeremy after requesting an interview with Nicholas alone and then returning almost immediately, she had no idea.

'Caitlin!'

The single word was undoubtedly a command. And quite instinctively, Caitlin swung to face him. He'd turned from the window and was looking into the room once more.

'What's wrong?' he asked.

'It's nothing.'

'Caitlin.' He sighed. 'Credit me with some sense of perception. Something troubled you sufficiently to drive you here to me. Tell me what it is.'

His expression had softened as he looked at her. He removed his hand from his pocket and strode towards her.

'Sit down, for goodness' sake. If it makes you feel any better, I'll sit with you.'

He almost pushed her down on to the settee and then sat down by the side of her. He placed one arm directly behind her upon the back of the settee.

She dug into her jacket pocket and brought out the small packet.

'It's this.'

She saw him frown as he looked down at it. He reached over and took it from her, studied it carefully for a moment. He tipped some of the white powder into the palm of one hand and with the index finger of the other, lifted some up and tasted it.

'Cocaine,' he said. He glanced back

at her, his gaze speculative now. 'Yours?'

'Of course it isn't mine. I'd hardly be likely to bring it to you if it was.'

'Then whose is it?'

'Donna's, I think.'

Nicholas shook his head, as if trying to clear it. He was obviously puzzled.

'I'm sorry, you'll have to be more explicit. Who is Donna?'

'David's girlfriend.'

'Aah, David's girlfriend. I see, or, at least, I think I do. Why have you brought it to me?'

'I wanted your advice on what I should do about it.'

'Well, call me stupid if you like, but why should you do anything about it?'

'I found it at my aunt's flat.'

'You'll have to explain again, Caitlin, I'm afraid. How did it get into your aunt's flat? Has David been round?'

'He's staying there. He and Donna, just for a while.'

Nicholas stared at her, thoughtfully.

'I'm worried that she might have persuaded David into using it, too. I can't tell Aunt Jessica, not at the moment.'

'What makes you so sure David isn't already using it?'

'I'm not sure, that's the problem. But if there's a possibility that he's not, then I want to prevent it happening. I found it among Donna's things, and it seemed to be hidden. If she's hiding it from David, the chances are that he doesn't know.'

'Yes, I see. Although it could just be hidden from you.'

'I'd thought of that, but they weren't to know I'd go to clean their room.'

Nicholas raised an eyebrow.

'That'll teach you to play housewife. Do you want me to talk to David? Is that why you're here?'

'Good grief, no. That would be the worst thing you could do. He's already partly convinced that it was you who stole . . . '

She stopped as she realised what she was saying.

'Stole the paintings? Is that what you

were about to say?' Nicholas got to his feet. 'I'd got wind of the accusations that Jessica had been making about my father, but that I should be accused as well?'

His expression was full of rage as he loomed over her. Caitlin pressed herself back against the settee. He was furious.

'Upon what does she and David base these preposterous assumptions?'

'The fact that you'd been in the shop the day the first painting went missing, and that you were alone in there for a moment or two. Nicholas, I just want to say that I don't . . . '

'And do you share these suspicions?' His lips curled in a knowing sneer. 'They are your family after all and, as such, I know you feel a great loyalty to them. You might as well finish what you've started. Tell me, do you think I'm the thief?'

'I don't know what to think if you want the truth,' she blurted out.

Nicholas's jaw squared as his lips tightened. She knew she was treading on very dangerous ground now but suddenly, she didn't care.

'You clearly know something that I don't,' she blundered on. 'Something that happened between your father and my aunt. Something serious enough to make my aunt think such a thing is possible.'

He stared at her, his anger seeming to dissipate as a curious expression invaded his good-looking face.

'Yet, doubting me as you obviously do, you come here for my advice. A bit ironic, isnt it?'

'Not really,' she bit back, finally driven to allowing her anger free rein.

She wanted to lash out at him, hurt him, as he was hurting her with his indifference, which was ridiculous when all she really wanted was to have him take her in his arms and hold her!

'I had no-one else to go to. You were as good as anyone.'

'Well, how flattering!' Nicholas retaliated sharply. 'Any port in a storm. Is that it? Or could it be this?'

Nicholas leaned down and with both hands dragged her to her feet. With one hand, he tossed the packet of cocaine to one side, on to the settee. He moved his hands up and grasped Caitlin by the shoulders.

In the next moment, he'd pulled her towards him. He stared down at her for a long moment, his eyes darkening as he lowered his head and his mouth claimed hers. Caitlin found herself responding as if her very life depended upon it.

Her shaking hands clung to him, holding on to him as her lips parted only too willingly beneath his. He gathered her closer, and she thought she heard him mutter, 'Caitlin, dear Caitlin.'

She was caught in the grip of a passion too powerful to resist. She could only moan softly as her pulses raced. Suddenly, Nicholas seemed to realise what was happening, and in the next moment, Caitlin found herself free. She could only stare helplessly up at him, lips quivering, too stricken to speak.

He returned her gaze for a long moment before saying, 'Here, take this and go.'

He picked up the small packet and thrust it at her.

'Nicholas, please, I didn't mean what I said.'

'Oh, but I think you did.'

His eyes were as cold as ice, the flames of his fury of passion cooled down in the aftermath of their kiss.

'Just go, Caitlin,' he repeated, and with these flat, toneless words, he turned away from her.

Caitlin walked slowly back to the gallery, trying desperately to come to terms with what she'd just discovered. She had fallen in love with Nicholas Millward! It was clear, humiliatingly clear, that Nicholas knew that she was hopelessly attracted to him. He'd always known.

His kiss and the words leading up to it had told her that. What it hadn't told her was, did he feel the same way? If he didn't, then the chances were that her opportunity to work with him was lost.

None of her thoughts explained why he'd kissed her in the first place, however. He'd been furiously angry with her. Was it his way of punishing her, for her implicit accusation? If that had been his intention, then he'd succeeded beyond his wildest dreams.

She'd have to hand in her notice now. They couldn't possibly work together, not after this.

When she reached the flat, David was there. His presence, as well as what he had to say, effectively drove all thoughts of Nicholas and that disturbing kiss from her mind, at least, for the moment. There was no sign of Donna.

'Have you been into our bedroom, Caitlin?' was David's first question.

'Yes, unfortunately,' she muttered. 'I found this, David, while I was dusting. It was hidden beneath a make-up pouch.'

She held out the packet, watching her

cousin's face closely all the time. He regarded it warily but said nothing, except for a disappointingly surly, 'You had no business to go in there. Where have you been with it?'

He looked scared, frightened that she might have done something rash, no doubt, which, now that she came to consider it, she supposed she had. Supposing Nicholas took it upon himself to go to the police?

'Oh, don't worry. Donna is safe enough. I won't go to the police with it, although, by rights, I suppose I should.'

She passed a hand that still trembled over her eyes. She was supposed to be resting, taking a holiday. Instead, she'd done her aunt a favour and now found herself caught up in some sort of family feud and, as if that weren't enough, now this incident with David.

David said nothing.

'You knew Donna had drugs then?' she asked.

He nodded, watching for her reaction.

'I haven't told your mother,' Caitlin said sternly, 'but if I ever suspect that you're using it, too, then, rest assured, I will.'

She suspected that David stood in more awe of his mother's cutting tongue than he ever would of the genial Sergeant Wilmot, especially as Jessica could, and probably would, cut off the very generous allowance she paid him, if she ever stumbled upon him doing such a thing.

When Caitlin checked David's and Donna's room the following morning, to her intense relief, there was no sign of the package. Donna hadn't returned either.

Later, when Caitlin asked David where she was, he merely said, 'She's gone back to her folks for a while. We thought it best.'

* * *

Two days later, Alan turned up!

It was late afternoon, and Caitlin was

just considering shutting up shop. She hadn't had a single customer all day and it hardly seemed worthwhile staying open on the off-chance that someone would come in. So, she was understandably surprised when, at the very moment that she had begun to walk to the door to drop the catch, Alan appeared.

'Why, Alan! What are you doing here?'

'What do you think?' he asked bluntly. 'I've come to talk to you.'

Caitlin contemplated him, uneasily. She'd never seen him look so determined.

He was very tanned, so clearly he'd gone ahead and flown out to the Seychelles. She had wondered at the time of her calling off if he'd still go on holiday without her.

'You look very well,' she began, in a futile attempt to ease the tension between them. 'Good holiday?'

It was the wrong thing to say. His features hardened.

'Yes, no thanks to you. That was a cruel thing you did, Caitlin.'

'I know.' She paused. 'I'm sorry, Alan, but the truth is I've known for some time now that we're not right for each other. It seemed an opportune moment to let you end things.'

'Oh, you've known for some time, have you? And you just decided you'd let it end?' he sneered.

'Yes. You're not in love with me. You just think you are.'

'Is that right? And tell me, Caitlin, as you're so very wise, how do you know what I feel?'

'I do, that's all.'

Alan glanced around the gallery.

'Where's the precious son and heir? Out on important business?'

Caitlin didn't bother dignifying that with an answer. It was evident that Alan didn't expect one because he went on, 'I want you to come back to me. Despite what you think you know, I want us to try again.'

'No, Alan, it wouldn't be any good.

You're infatuated with me. If you'd give yourself some breathing space, you'd realise it, too. You deserve someone better.'

'I want you, Caitlin. Don't you know what you've done to me? Can't you see?'

'I'm beginning to,' Caitlin began gently, 'but, believe me, Alan, if you'd only consider things rationally.'

'Are you calling me irrational?'

'No, not exactly.'

Alan strode towards her, his expression a threatening one. Caitlin took a step back. A glint of satisfaction showed on his face. This wasn't the Alan that she knew. He would never have tried to frighten her in such a manner.

'Alan, don't do anything silly.'

'I will do anything, say anything, to convince you that you're meant for me.'

He reached for her, but Caitlin managed to evade him, positioning herself so that a low table stood between them.

'Of course, that's it, isn't it?' He

spoke in a low voice. 'There's someone else?' He glanced scornfully round the shop. 'All this was just an excuse to end things between us. You knew if you backed out of the holiday at the very last moment what the outcome would be, didn't you?'

'No, Alan, that's not true. Aunt Jessica needed me here. She's still in hospital. And as for your other remark, no, there isn't anyone else.'

Her lie made her feel ashamed, but she knew it would help neither of them at this point if she was truthful. She would just hurt Alan even more than he was already hurting.

'Alan, please listen to me.'

'No. I've done with listening to you. I'll make you love me, Caitlin. I know you've never felt about me as I feel about you but I also know, given time, you will. We just need time.'

'No, you're deluding yourself, Alan,' she broke in, her voice sharp.

It was no good, however. Alan wasn't in any mood to be reasoned with and much as she hated having to hurt him any more than she already had, she knew, that for him as well as for herself, it would be the best thing in the long run.

'I will never love you, Alan, and, if you'd only admit it, you don't love me.'

For the first time, he seemed to be listening to her. She felt a cautious optimism.

'Think about it, about your real feelings. You've never felt real passion for me, have you?'

'Oh, I see.' His lips curled at her. 'It's passion that's missing, is it? Well, if it's passion you want, I'll give you passion.'

He strode round the table and made a grab for her. This time, he managed to get hold of her. Caitlin tried to struggle free, with the result that they began to stagger about the shop. She heard the tinkle of china as they knocked an ornament off the table.

'Alan,' she cried, 'for goodness' sake.'

But Alan's mouth cut off her next words as he began to force himself upon her, bringing his mouth down on hers. His back was to the door, with Caitlin on his other side, so, not only could she not see the door, she didn't even hear it opening, or see the man who gazed in amazement at the couple who appeared to be locked in a passionate embrace.

The man stood silently in the doorway, his steely gaze going from the couple to the overturned table. His lip curled, before he whirled around and, quietly closing the door behind him once more, strode off along the street.

When Caitlin finally succeeded in freeing herself, all she could do was gasp.

'Get out, Alan. Just go. I never want to see you again.'

Alan's face was the colour of chalk as he muttered, 'I'm sorry, but you asked for that.'

'I didn't ask you for anything. Now just go.' And with that, she swung away from him, bending down to right the table and then start picking up the pieces of broken china. 'I have some clearing up to do.'

Next morning, Caitlin walked into the shop from the stock-room to find Nicholas standing in front of the small Landseer painting. Her heart leaped but, in the next second, he had turned to face her and what she discerned there, in the slate grey eyes, was enough to make her stomach lurch.

'I want to talk to you,' he said, without preamble of any kind. 'I called yesterday afternoon, but you were otherwise occupied.'

'Yesterday afternoon?' Caitlin stammered. 'What time? I didn't see you.'

'No, as I said, you were already occupied.'

Caitlin's breath caught in her throat. He must have called while Alan was with her! He must have seen them!

'I see you comprehend my meaning. Your lover, was it?' he drawled.

'No.'

'No?' Nicholas's eyebrow rose in the manner with which she was becoming so familiar. 'Do you treat all your male acquaintances with such generosity? I'll have to remember that,' he concluded drily, 'and not allow myself to be so misled by you in the future.'

Deciding that all she could do was disregard the sarcastic remark, she interrupted with the admirably impartial, 'I'm glad you've come in, Nicholas. I have something for you.'

Her shame at the manner in which he looked at her then coloured her cheeks scarlet.

'Well, well, I wonder what that can be,' he murmured suggestively. 'I really think I'll have to pass this time, Caitlin, as charming as your offer may be.'

She thrust the letter she had written at him. She had been carrying it in anticipation of just such an encounter as this. It should express her feelings about everything that had happened between them, she judged. It was her resignation.

Nicholas, however, didn't react as she had expected him to. But then, she sighed, when did he ever do what was expected of him? He glanced down at the envelope, and making no move to open it, demanded, 'What's this?'

'Open it and you'll find out.'

Nicholas tore it open. His face revealed nothing as he read its contents. He then strode to the waste bin and tore the note into shreds before dropping the pieces into the basket.

'Why have you done that? Haven't you read it properly?' Caitlin demanded angrily.

'Of course I read it properly. You saw me doing so. I just don't accept it, that's all.'

'But after the other day,' she mumbled, thoroughly embarrassed now as she looked away from his amused scrutiny, 'we can't possibly work together. I thought — isn't that why you're here?'

'No.'

His expression softened fractionally as he regarded her.

'If what happened between us is

what's been worrying you, forget it. I have. I won't tell the boyfriend. Promise! I'm not one to place an exaggerated importance on a few, casual kisses.'

Caitlin did flinch. He considered her cheap, too free with her kisses. He'd dismissed their embraces with an ease that appalled her. Why couldn't she do the same?

'Then — then — why are you here?' she asked finally, when she'd pulled herself together and regained some semblance of self-control.

'My father and I have had a long talk and he's given me permission to go ahead and tell you what happened between your aunt and him. In other words, that you should know the truth.'

'Truth? What truth?'

'That Jessica jilted him, practically at the altar.'

7

Caitlin stared incredulously at Nicholas. 'What?' she spluttered, puzzling unsuccessfully as to what was to be revealed.

'You heard, Caitlin.'

'Well, yes, I did,' Caitlin admitted faintly, 'but, frankly, I'm stunned. I didn't know they'd ever been connected in that way. I knew there must be something more than my aunt was telling me, naturally. But I never for a moment suspected this. Why has she never said anything?'

'Too ashamed, I shouldn't wonder. After all, it's not something one broadcasts, is it?' Nicholas retorted. 'It had been a whirlwind romance from what my father has told me. They'd met and planned to marry all within the space of six months. However, three days before the wedding, your aunt met up with David's father, whom she'd known a couple of years previously it seemed. It was love at second sight,' he remarked sardonically, 'and instead of standing at the altar taking her vows with my father, she married William Haydock.'

Suddenly, all the incomprehensible, little pieces fell into place for Caitlin.

'So that's why she thinks Jeremy bears her a grudge. It's nothing to do with the buying of the Orion, as she's always maintained. But, Nicholas, if her theory were right, and Jeremy does bear her a grudge, then his losing the gallery to her would just have increased his anger and resentment.'

'Precisely. The facts, though, whatever your aunt would like to believe, are that Jeremy doesn't really bear her a grudge. Jessica simply chooses to believe that. In fact, she actually needs to believe it in my view. If she could prove that it was Jeremy who was behind the thefts, it would bear her theory out.'

Caitlin sat down as Nicholas went on.

'All these years later, your aunt still feels guilty over what she did to my father and, I suppose, in a roundabout way, his supposed crimes would alleviate those feelings. Jeremy would have revenged himself and the slate would be wiped clean. As it happens, she doesn't need to feel guilt.

'My father met my mother not long afterwards and fell deeply in love. He has since admitted that he and your aunt would never have been suited. And knowing your aunt, as I have come to do over the years, I have to agree with him.' Nicholas's words were scathing.

'But, all that must have happened some thirty-five years ago,' Caitlin said.

'Thirty-six, actually. Rather a long time for anyone to carry a grudge, wouldn't you say?' Nicholas's smile was tight-lipped.

'Does Jessica have any idea that Jeremy feels that way? That they wouldn't have suited?'

The notion had occurred to her that her aunt had, and still did, possibly, resent Jeremy falling in love so swiftly after her departure from his life and that was why she was so eager to blame him now, all these years later, for the thefts.

'No. Why would she? It's none of her business.'

'So,' Caitlin said slowly, trying to get things straight in her own mind, 'you think that she wants to believe Jeremy is having his revenge, to make herself feel better about what she did all those years ago?'

'Yes. I really can't think of any other reason for her to all but accuse him — or me — of the thefts. She must know she's barking up the wrong tree. If she had a shred of evidence to substantiate it all she would have given it to the police.'

'I think what fuelled her suspicions of your father was the fact that nothing's been stolen from the Pimpernel.'

Caitlin watched Nicholas closely as she spoke.

'Who told her that? Of course we've had things stolen. What shop doesn't these days? Nothing as valuable as what Jessica has had taken, I'll grant you, but, nonetheless, we have our problems with shop-lifting, too.'

'Does Jeremy know that she suspects one of you?' Caitlin went on to ask.

'No. I couldn't see any point in telling him. It would only distress him, as well as infuriate him if he thought the finger of suspicion was being pointed at me as well. As far as he's concerned, it's all long forgotten. I can't see the point in provoking open warfare between them, because that's what it would mean. My father might seem the gentlest of men, but in actual fact, he's got one heck of a temper when provoked.'

Caitlin suspected that his son had one also but she refrained from saying so. At that moment, the phone in the back room rang.

'Oh, excuse me for a second.'

'It's OK. I've said what I came for. I'll go now.' His voice was cold, as cold as his expression as he looked at her.

'Yes right — fine.'

Caitlin watched him stride towards the shop door with a sense of hopelessness. He seemed to despise her. The insistent ringing of the telephone dragged her thoughts back to business and she turned and went into the storeroom.

It was one of the gallery's suppliers checking on an order for a particular frame that Jessica had given him before her heart attack and it was while Caitlin was talking to him that she thought she heard the shop door open again.

'Just a moment, please. Someone's come in.'

But the man on the other end wouldn't stop talking. It was several minutes before Caitlin managed to break free and hurry into the shop to see who had come in.

Her first thought had been that it was

Nicholas returning to say something else, but there was no-one there. Deciding that she must have imagined the sound, she returned to the call on the telephone.

It wasn't until later that afternoon, when she was dusting all the pictures, that she noticed the Landseer was missing from the wall! The empty hook stared accusingly at her. She gazed incredulously at the space. That had been the painting that Nicholas had been looking at when she'd walked into the shop and found him there.

Frantically, she cast her mind back through the morning's customers. There had been several and, of course, there had been what had sounded like the opening of the shop door while she'd been on the phone. Someone must have come in, taken the painting off the wall, and then made their escape. There was no other explanation. She hadn't left the shop again after the phone call.

Caitlin called the police. The sergeant, when he arrived, wanted to know just who had been in the shop that day. Caitlin had to name Nicholas, amongst others. Sergeant Wilmot looked at her, thoughtfully.

'Nicholas Millward seems to come in here a lot, which is rather strange when you come to think of it, seeing as how his father also owns an art gallery. I seem to recall his name being mentioned on the occasion of the first theft.'

'Oh, sergeant, I don't think . . . '

She had to prevent him from going to see either of the Millward men. It would be just like Nicholas to think that Caitlin had deliberately set the policeman on to him.

'I'm sorry, miss. I know it seems unlikely that a gentleman in Mr Millward's position would do such a thing but I have to explore every avenue. You do understand?'

'Yes, of course.'

She had a very heavy heart when she went to see her aunt that evening and told her what had happened. Caitlin felt that she'd let her aunt down, although, in no way, could she be blamed.

'You say Nicholas Millward had been in?' Jessica immediately asked when Caitlin told her what had happened.

'It wasn't Nicholas who took it, Aunt Jessica. I would stake my life on that.'

'And that's proof of his innocence? Your readiness to throw your life away? For goodness' sake, Caitlin, don't be naive. That's twice now that a painting has gone missing on the same day that he's been in. Coincidence? I don't think so.'

Caitlin hadn't been going to tell her aunt that she knew what had happened between her and Jeremy Millward all those years ago, or at least, not yet. However, her aunt seemed considerably stronger than she had been a couple of days ago, her colour almost back to normal, and she was sitting up in bed.

'Nicholas had come in specifically to see me,' Caitlin said, deciding she couldn't bear to see Nicholas blamed a moment longer.

Jessica stared down her nose at her niece.

'You getting involved with him, Caitlin? Take my advice, my dear, and don't.'

'I know the truth, Aunt.'

'Truth?' Jessica's tone was brusque. 'What truth? What are you talking about?'

'About you and Jeremy Millward and what happened all those years ago.'

'Oh, you do, do you? Couldn't keep his mouth shut, eh? Well, you know now why the pair of them are doing this to me. It's revenge, retribution, call it what you will. I humiliated Jeremy before all his fine friends and he's never forgiven me.'

'What I can't understand is why no-one has ever mentioned your engagement to me. Not you, not my mother. Yet, she must have known.'

'Did the subject ever come up with your mother, Caitlin?'

'Well, no.'

144

'There you are then. It all happened eight or nine years before you were born. There was no need to mention it. Knowing your mother, she'd probably forgotten all about it anyway.'

'She did say once that you had been engaged for a while to someone else. I'd never given it another thought.'

Her aunt made no reply to this.

'It's not true, you know, about Jeremy not forgiving you, Aunt. He forgave you a long time ago,' Caitlin put in quietly.

'Told you that, did he?' snapped Jessica.

'Well, no, but Nicholas did.'

'Hah! Nicholas. What does he know? It was before he was born as well.'

'Nicholas knows quite a lot about it, apparently. His father has been honest with him. Jeremy has been very happy with his wife, Nicholas's mother. There'd be no reason for him to bear a grudge.'

'Nicholas told you that, too, no doubt?'

'Yes.'

'Well, what did you expect him to say? That they'd been miserable? Anyway, why did he come and tell you all this?'

Jessica was eyeing Caitlin with suspicion now.

Caitlin paused. She couldn't tell her aunt about finding the drugs and having to ask Nicholas for advice, which had been what had led up to Nicholas being forced to tell her the truth.

'It just sort of came up,' she said lamely.

'Hah! Came up? You were being nosy. Did you tell him what I've been thinking about him and his father?' Jessica could be very shrewd at times.

'He guessed.' Caitlin hesitated. 'He's heard certain rumours.'

Jessica looked appalled for a second.

'Oh, no! What did he say?'

Caitlin shrugged. She had no intention of alarming her aunt with the truth about the extent of Nicholas's fury.

'Although, I suppose it could stop

any more thefts taking place,' Jessica continued.

'Aunt Jessica,' Caitlin said as she felt irritation at her aunt's refusal to see the irrationality of her suspicions, 'Nicholas and his father wouldn't stoop to what you accuse them of.'

'Don't be so naive, Caitlin. Jeremy Millward has never forgiven me, despite what his fool of a son says. He hasn't forgiven me for jilting him and for snatching the Orion Gallery from beneath his nose.'

'Nicholas is far from being a fool, Aunt Jessica, and, anyway, it happened thirty-six years ago. No-one holds a grudge for that long. Why would he have waited until now to get his own back? Will you tell me that?'

'Because,' Jessica snapped, exasperated that she thought her niece was being deliberately obstructive, 'it's only now that he's got the opportunity. While William was alive, there was nothing he could do, and I didn't own the gallery then. My beating him to it simply added to his sense of grievance. Jeremy was always a proud man. His son has got the same streak.'

'So why would they stoop to stealing? Surely that very pride that you're so scathing about would prevent them from doing such a thing? None of it would make sense in any case, even if it were Jeremy. You're insured against theft, aren't you?'

'No, not any more.'

'What?' Caitlin was aghast.

'The insurance company refused to renew the policy after the last theft. They also refused to pay out more than a nominal sum at the time. They want me to install a security system with a hidden camera, grills over the windows, a direct line to the police, all that nonsense. It would have cost a fortune. I'd rather spend it on stock for the shop.'

'But you haven't spent it on stock, have you? I wondered why there were no paintings of any note in the gallery, apart from the Landseer.'

'I've been waiting for the right ones to come along. And now they have.'

Caitlin ignored that last statement for the moment.

'But, Aunt Jessica, you can't have valuable paintings on the walls if you're not covered against their theft by some form of insurance. Supposing they're stolen as well?'

'I'll take good care this time that they're not.'

Caitlin tried again to make her aunt see sense.

'Wouldn't it be better to use whatever money you've still got to install a security system?'

'Then that wouldn't leave me anything with which to buy paintings. What use would a sophisticated security system be if there's nothing in the shop to steal? You can see the predicament I'm in, Caitlin. It makes more sense, for the present, to buy the paintings. Then I can sell them, hopefully make enough money to restock the shop on a regular basis and install the security system. Do you see? I get the best of both worlds that way.'

Caitlin thought Jessica was being unduly optimistic. What if she bought some more paintings, didn't sell them straight away, and then, despite the precautions she took, they were stolen? She'd be right back where she started, and with no funds left.

But it was no good. No amount of persuasion would convince Aunt Jessica what she was risking. She was adamant.

'Now, listen to me, Caitlin,' she went on eagerly, 'there's an auction coming up and there are two paintings I want you to go along and bid for. I should make enough of a profit on their re-sale to do all that I've mentioned. Now, I've a good idea what they'll go for so I've signed a blank cheque for you. I know Jeremy will want them. He mustn't get them. I don't care what you have to pay, buy them. Do you understand, Caitlin?'

'But if I have to pay too much, Aunt Jessica, there'll be no room left to make a profit on their re-sale.'

'You leave me to worry about that, my girl. You just make sure you buy them. Now, there should be enough money left in my account to cover them. If they go over what I'm expecting, well, the bank manager's a good friend. He won't bounce the cheque. He'll stand the difference.'

'Are you sure?' Caitlin couldn't disguise her anxiety. 'How much do you think I'll have to give for them?'

Her aunt named a price that had Caitlin gasping.

'But if it's all the money you've got left, isn't that taking rather too much of a risk? Couldn't I just buy one of them?'

'No. I want you to get them both.' The older woman was becoming agitated. 'I'm not allowing that rogue Millward to beat me.'

She fell back on her pillows, gasping for breath.

'Caitlin, promise me you'll get them. Promise.'

Caitlin, thoroughly alarmed at her aunt's

reaction, hastened to reassure her.

'All right, Aunt Jessica, I promise. Don't worry.'

'Don't forget, I want both of them. I'll manage about the money, you'll see.'

Caitlin left, convinced that no matter what she or anyone else said to the contrary, Jessica was becoming increasingly obsessed with what she saw as the ongoing battle between herself and Jeremy Millward.

Buying the two paintings at the prices her aunt suggested would clean out her bank account. But whatever Caitlin herself thought, she knew she had no choice but to do what her aunt demanded. Her aunt, despite the slight improvement, was still too weak to be unduly agitated by being contradicted.

So, on the following Monday, Caitlin found herself amongst the other bidders for the two paintings — Lots 28 and 29. Lot 28 was by a well-known artist, but Lot 29, an extremely large and ornately-framed oil painting, was by an artis completely unknown to Caitlin.

She had been on the look-out for Jeremy's arrival but was horrified to see Nicholas stride in instead. What was he doing here? He should be hard at work at Gallagher's! He didn't see Caitlin and she tried very hard to stay out of view by positioning herself behind a pillar.

She couldn't resist a peek, however, to see just where Nicholas had positioned himself for the bidding. Because, as her aunt had predicted, Nicholas could only be here for the same reason as Caitlin.

Just as she poked her head out, as luck would have it, Nicholas turned. It was obvious he had seen her because his gaze narrowed speculatively as it rested upon the pillar behind which she remained concealed. He would know that there was a good chance that she would be bidding against him. There would be no other reason for her to be here.

Caitlin's throat was dry as the

bidding began for the first of the two paintings, the better-known water colour. It began at ten thousand pounds, and as Caitlin had anticipated, she found herself bidding against several people, one of whom was Nicholas. However, the other prospective buyers soon dropped out once the price began to climb, until it was just Caitlin and Nicholas.

As the price went up and up, sweat broke out on Caitlin's brow. Jessica had grossly underestimated the price it would go for. Caitlin prayed that her aunt's bank manager would live up to Jessica's expectations because if he didn't and the second painting went for as much again, she was in deep trouble.

Nicholas seemed as determined to get the painting as Caitlin was but just as Caitlin was weighing up the possibility of disobeying her aunt and dropping out, Nicholas suddenly stopped bidding and the painting was knocked down to Caitlin.

She drew a steadying breath but then had to go through precisely the same thing again with the second painting. Then, as before, Nicholas drove the price up and then quite simply dropped out. The second painting also went to Caitlin. She was on her way out of the door afterwards when his familiar voice sounded from behind her.

'Caitlin, I want to talk to you.'

'Look, I'm sorry that you didn't get at least one of the paintings,' she said apologetically.

'It's not the paintings I want to discuss. You've had another painting stolen, I believe.'

Caitlin could only nod.

'On the very day I called in to see you? Saturday.'

Once again, Caitlin found herself nodding, bereft of words.

'And you sent Sergeant Wilmot to question me. You really do believe it was me, don't you?'

'No, Nicholas, of course I don't and I'm sorry that's the impression I gave you. Your cynical comment the day I came to the Pimpernel, about my loyalty to my family, annoyed me and, regretfully, I allowed that to lead me into saying things I didn't mean. For that I apologise.

'I've never believed that either you or your father was responsible for the thefts, and I didn't send Sergeant Wilmot to question you. He asked me who had been into the gallery that day and I had to tell him. If he'd discovered later that you'd been there, it would have looked more suspicious than if I hadn't said anything. I'm sorry, but I didn't know what else to do.'

'No.' Nicholas's tone was grudging. 'I suppose you had no choice. By the way, you've paid well over the odds for those two paintings today. It's very unlikely that Jessica will recoup the cost on a re-sale, let alone make a profit.'

'Jessica seems confident that she'll make a profit on them,' Caitlin said, trying to sound confident.

'Well, good luck to her then. Does she have a buyer in mind?'

Caitlin simply shrugged. It appeared

to her then that Nicholas was fishing for information. She changed the subject. 'How are things going at Gallagher's?'

'Fine. It'll be a whole lot easier, of course, when you're back. Shouldn't be long now, should it? Your month must be almost up.'

'Not quite. I've got eight days left yet,' she replied. 'I would have thought you'd be there today actually. Patrick grant you the day off, did he?' she asked, with a wicked smile

'We agreed I wouldn't be needed for a day or two. I've left them all with more than enough work to do. Delegation, Caitlin, that's the secret of good management.' He paused before going on. 'Well, I must go. I'll see you in eight days, if not before,' and with that, he casually strolled away.

It wasn't until later that she considered what Nicholas had said about the paintings.

'You've paid well over the odds,' he'd said, which meant, that if their roles had been reversed and it had been

Caitlin who had dropped out, he would have paid over the odds also. Had Nicholas deliberately driven the price up, guessing that her aunt, in her search for a victory over Jeremy, would have instructed Caitlin to get the two paintings at any cost? He would know that it would leave Jessica seriously out of pocket, the gallery vulnerable and at risk, and with no chance of selling either of the overpriced paintings.

She might have no choice then but to sell to Jeremy or anyone else who would buy. It was a disturbing thought but it was one which Caitlin found herself powerless to dismiss. It was exactly the kind of way in which Nicholas would work. He wouldn't need to resort to stealing. He could ruin her aunt and stay well within the boundaries of the law. Is that what he'd just done?

Fortunately, the bank manager agreed to the extra money needed to cover the cheque, as Jessica had predicted. It did leave Jessica owing an uncomfortably large amount of money to the bank, however. They really needed to sell the two paintings, or at least one, and quickly. Yet, if Nicholas were to be believed, that could prove very difficult, if not impossible.

Caitlin was determined to take every precaution she could, to prevent anyone stealing the two valuable additions to the gallery. She had managed to get the larger oil painting into the window, estimating that it was too big for anyone to simply walk into the shop and lift it out while her back was turned.

The smaller water colour she'd hung on the wall immediately behind the counter where she could keep a close watch on it, even when she was on the phone. If either of them should go missing, then bankruptcy would be staring Jessica in the face. There was no doubt of that.

With no painting to sell and no insurance money to be claimed, it would be the end of the Orion Gallery, at least under Jessica's ownership. She wouldn't be able to pay back the bank, and, no matter how understanding the bank manager, that meant almost certain trouble.

With all this in mind, Caitlin resolved to take the smaller painting upstairs with her at night and to lock the bigger one into the store-room.

David had called in while she had been debating where to hang them.

'Very nice,' he commented, gazing down at them still leaning against the wall. 'Are these the two that were up for auction?'

'Yes. They've just arrived.'

David had moved out of the flat above the shop and he and Donna had moved into another flat together. This meant that Caitlin was once more alone at the gallery.

'I won't be leaving them in the shop overnight, David. I intend taking every precaution I can. We can't afford to have these stolen.'

It wasn't until she saw the strange way in which David was regarding her that the thought occurred to her that he mightn't know that the gallery was no longer covered by an insurance policy. She decided to say nothing more on the subject.

Instead, she murmured, 'Who knows when something else worth having will come along?'

'No, quite.' It was obvious that David accepted her explanation. 'What are you going to do with them then?'

'I'll take the smaller one to bed with me, so to speak.' She smiled at David's surprised expression. 'The bigger one I'll lock securely in the store-room.'

'Good idea. Can't be too careful with what's already happened. Mum told me the small Landseer had gone, after Millward had been in again. If he gets wind of what we've got here, he'll probably have a go at laying his hands on them as well.'

Caitlin didn't respond to this. She still couldn't bring herself to believe that Nicholas bore her aunt such ill will. She knew that Nicholas wouldn't have stolen the Landseer and there was probably a perfectly reasonable explanation for his driving the auction prices up.

Perhaps he had wanted the paintings for his own private collection. Yes, of course, that was it. Why hadn't she thought of that before? It wouldn't matter then if the price was too high. He wasn't looking to make a profit on them, at least, not in the near future. He might want to sell them eventually, by which time, knowing the art world, their value would have gone up anyway.

Jessica herself would be unlikely to make a profit on their re-sale but at least it would ensure that she could pay off the bank.

'You look worn out, David. Been working or something?' Caitlin had been so preoccupied with her thoughts, she had only just noticed the wearied look to her cousin.

'No. Donna and I have been to a couple of all-night parties. A good night's sleep will soon put me to rights.

Listen, I might have a buyer for one of these pictures.'

'Oh, really. Aunt Jessica would be pleased if we could sell one of them.'

'I'll see what I can do. Where are you displaying them?'

'Well, I thought the big one in the window and the smaller one here, behind the counter.'

'Great. They'll look good. I'll try to coax the prospective buyer in then, to see them.'

That evening, Caitlin locked up and with slight difficulty, eventually lifted the larger picture out of the window. It had been much easier to get it in, she mused. She carried the smaller one straight upstairs, but the bigger one, as she had expected, was more difficult to handle.

She locked it securely in the small store-room. It had only one window and that was barred. Perhaps it had been used previously to store items of particular value. Whatever, knowing it was in there would enable her to sleep more peacefully than if she had left it in full view of any passer-by in the shop window.

She was in bed and asleep when the sound of glass breaking and the shop's burglar alarm startled her. Her first instinct was to call the police, but then, knowing that they would most likely take several minutes to arrive on the scene, by which time the thief or thieves would have got away with the painting, she decided to take her life in her hands and go down and take a look herself.

At best, it could be a false alarm; at worst, it could be thieves who would take one look at her and hopefully take to their heels, without the precious painting.

Quickly, she found the key to the store-room and, picking up a heavy torch, which she had been keeping by the bed, just in case, she descended the stairs. Perhaps she ought to make a noise. That way, they would hear her coming and hopefully make their escape before she got there.

Which was what she thought had happened when she saw the smashed front window but no sign of anyone in the shop. Breathing a sigh of relief, she ran to the door of the store-room. She'd got the key in her hand ready to unlock it when something heavy struck her from behind.

When she eventually opened her eyes again, it was to find herself looking directly up into Nicholas Millward's face! And standing right behind him was David and behind him, a uniformed policeman.

8

Nicholas was crouched down by the side of Caitlin, both hands grasping her by the shoulders, his face as white as she imagined hers must be. 'What happened?' he asked anxiously.

'Someone hit me from behind.'

Caitlin winced as she touched the back of her head. There was already a sizeable lump but luckily the skin didn't feel broken.

'Oh, no, the painting. Is the painting still there? In the storeroom?'

Weakly, she pointed to where she knew the door was.

'Don't worry about the painting,' Nicholas ordered curtly. 'It's insured.'

'But that's just it, Nicholas, it isn't!' She groaned. 'Neither of them was.'

'What?' David exclaimed, coming now to stand just behind Nicholas. 'What do you mean?' David looked stricken.

'The insurance company wouldn't go on providing cover against theft unless Jessica had closed circuit television, expensive window grills, and other safeguards. David, is the painting still in the store-room? Please, go and look. My key must be on the floor over there. I had it in my hand when I was knocked out.'

'No need of a key. The door's wide open, and there's nothing in there, Caitlin. I've already looked. The thief must have waited for you to come down, knocked you out and then used your key to open the door and take the painting.'

Nicholas lifted his head.

'He was mighty quick off the mark then because I must have been here within minutes of the alarm going off and the window was smashed and the door open then. What size was the painting? Was it the big one?'

'Yes,' Caitlin murmured.

'And the thieves supposedly man-handled that out of a small room, got it through the broken window and into some sort of vehicle, whereupon they made their escape, all unseen and all within minutes of the alarm going off? It's not possible.'

Nicholas turned to look at the police constable.

'That painting, constable, must have measured at least three feet by four.'

'Here's your key, Caitlin,' David interrupted. 'It was on the floor.'

'David,' Caitlin said, 'go upstairs and see if the other painting is still in my bedroom.'

David ran off, returning within moments to say, 'The other one is still there.'

A tear edged its way from beneath Caitlin's eyelid.

'Caitlin, it's not your fault,' Nicholas urged. 'You did everything you could to keep the paintings safe. Just lie still. The doctor's on his way.'

'If I could just have a word with Miss Mortimer.' It was the young policeman inching his way forward.

'Not now, constable.' Nicholas's tone was unexpectedly brusque. 'The girl's hurt. She's had a severe shock. Why don't you question David Haydock? Someone must have had a key to get in in the first place, despite what all this looks like.'

'What on earth are you implying, Millward?' David demanded.

'Just that no more than three or four minutes could have elapsed between the time I heard the alarm going off and my getting here.'

'Well,' David snarled, 'if we're going to be asking questions, here's one for you, Millward. What were you doing before I got here and the constable arrived? That on its own is mighty suspicious in my book.'

'David, Nicholas, please, don't,' Caitlin began.

The two men ignored her. Nicholas straightened, having gently laid Caitlin back on to the floor again.

'How did you know it was this place being robbed anyway, Millward? What have you done? Stashed the painting away, ready for picking up later?'

Nicholas was clearly striving for calm in the face of David's preposterous suggestions. When he did finally speak, it was in a voice that was rigorously controlled and totally even.

'I was leaving my father's house when I heard the alarm. I drove straight to the village to check out whose it was and saw the broken window and Caitlin lying inside. I climbed in and called the police. How did you turn up, Haydock?'

David looked uncomfortable.

'I decided to come and check that everything was all right. After all the robberies we've had and knowing the new paintings were here, I dunno, I just felt uneasy, I suppose. Especially knowing Caitlin was here alone. Donna and I had been out and I dropped her back at the flat and walked here. As I got nearer, I could hear the alarm. Anything else you'd like to know?'

Nicholas appeared to lose patience

with the younger man. He reached out and caught him by his shirt collar, dragging him in towards him.

'I've made this my business, Haydock, because . . . '

'Constable,' David yelled, genuinely alarmed now by the expression of menace upon Nicholas's face, 'are you going to stand by and watch him beat me up?'

'Gentlemen, please.' It was the doctor. 'As riveting as all this is, could you delay things until I've had a look at the young lady?'

Nicholas turned instantly to see Caitlin standing to one side of him. If her face had been pale before, it was chalk white now. Her eyes were dark pools of anguish.

'Caitlin! I'm sorry. Are you OK?' He caught hold of her just as she swayed forwards. 'Caitlin, sweet . . . '

Caitlin, terrified that Nicholas and David were actually going to come to blows, had somehow managed to struggle to her feet. The effort proved too much for her, however, and she practically fell into Nicholas's open arms. Very, very gently, he lowered her to the floor, re-arranging the jacket he had positioned beneath her head before she regained consciousness.

Caitlin stared at him, everything else forgotten but the single question that hammered at her. What had Nicholas been going to say then? It had sounded perilously like 'sweetheart.'

'Caitlin,' Nicholas went on, 'stay still and see what the doctor has to say, then I'll get you upstairs to bed.'

'Oh, no, you will not,' David interrupted furiously. 'I'll see that my cousin gets to bed, thank you. I've heard enough tales about you and your affairs.'

Nicholas stood again and turned on David.

'If you don't want your blasted teeth knocked out, I suggest you keep quiet.'

His expression told David, in no uncertain terms, that he meant what he said. David, with a great show of reluctance, lapsed into silence.

'Now, young lady,' the doctor said to Caitlin, 'let's have a look at you, shall we?'

As the doctor made a thorough examination of Caitlin, she could hear the constable questioning Nicholas and David in the background. He clearly learned nothing of any value from either of them because he left soon afterwards, saying that he'd be back in the morning with the fingerprinting crew and nothing was to be touched till then.

Caitlin was ordered by the doctor to stay in bed for a couple of days at least. She assured him that she would be more than happy to do so. Her head ached abominably and several bruises were beginning to appear upon her body, obviously from when she'd fallen after being knocked out.

She felt guilty at being forced to leave the shop closed, never more so than when her aunt walked into her bedroom the next day. The older woman still looked very pale but there was a forceful determination to her that reassured Caitlin and prevented her from dealing too severely with her.

'Aunt, Jessica, what on earth are you doing here? You should still be in hospital.'

'Oh, do be quiet, Caitlin. What does it look as if I'm doing here? I couldn't lie in that hospital bed another day. Not after hearing about you being knocked out in my shop, trying to guard my property.'

'Who told you that?'

'Well, David did, of course. Who else?'

'Oh, Aunt Jessica, I asked him not to. I didn't want to worry you.' The tears began to roll again. She felt so weak and helpless. 'I'm sorry about the painting.'

At that, she began to quietly cry.

'Now you'll be ruined, with no insurance.' She began to grope beneath her pillow for the hankie that she knew was there somewhere.

'No, I won't be.' Jessica's tone was brisk and unconcerned. 'The painting's been returned. It's downstairs now.'

Caitlin stopped crying instantly. She gazed at her aunt, wide-eyed.

'But — but . . . ' She scrubbed at her eyes with the handkerchief she had finally located. 'I don't understand. Do you mean the police caught the thief?'

'No, not exactly. It's a long story, Caitlin.' She nervously eyed her niece. 'Oh well, I can see I'm going to have to explain.'

'Yes, indeed you are,' Caitlin insisted.

'It was David. He's been a very stupid boy but at least he's done the honourable thing and confessed.'

'David! You mean the robbery was down to David?'

'Yes, and all the other thefts. I haven't been as honest with you as I should have been. You remember that first painting that was stolen?'

Caitlin nodded as her aunt continued.

'Well, it wasn't me who was in the

shop at the time. It was David. He tells me he slipped the painting to Donna and she simply walked away with it. Foolishly, I believed him when he told me it must have been Nicholas. He's managed to get himself mixed up with some very nasty people who've even been giving him drugs, and he kept needing more and more money. That's why he took the paintings, to sell.'

Caitlin told her aunt of her discovery of the packet of cocaine but decided not to mention going to Nicholas with it.

'But, he'd have raised enough money from those first three paintings to have kept themselves supplied with drugs for years to come.'

'No. He was forced to accept a fraction of what the paintings were worth, simply because they were stolen.'

'Oh, I see.'

'He said you told him what you intended to do with the paintings the other night so, on the spur of the moment, he and a friend planned the break-in. He believed I was still insured so I'd get the money back. When you said that these last two weren't covered, he said he couldn't see his mother ruined so he confessed.'

'Was it David who knocked me out?'

'No, that was his so-called friend. They took care not to hit you too hard apparently, just enough to render you unconscious, although their actions were, unforgivable.

'David has keys to both the gallery and the store-room. So he let himself into the shop, turned off the alarm, unlocked the store-room and passed the painting to his accomplice who had a van outside. David then relocked the door, turned the alarm back on and went outside, locking the door again behind him. They then broke in to make it look like an ordinary burglary.

'David, knowing how concerned you were about the painting, guessed that when you heard the alarm you wouldn't wait for the police to arrive and would come down in an effort to frighten the burglars off yourself. It was a reckless gamble upon their parts, but one that sadly paid off, at the time, because, of course, my brave but foolhardy niece, that's exactly what you did.

'The friend knocked you out, David unlocked the store-room door with your key and they left. He'd planned to return, as if he'd simply heard the alarm, to discover you unconscious, when he would then have called the police.'

'But why go to those lengths. Why not just break in and take the painting?' Caitlin asked in bewilderment.

'They wouldn't have had time to make it look as if the store-room door had been forced, get the painting out and into the van before someone heard the alarm and called the police. If David had simply used his keys, we would have known who had done it. So, he made it look as if the burglar had waited for you to come down, knocked you out, and then used your key to unlock the storeroom door.'

'But they could have been caught while they were waiting for me.'

'I know. As I said, it was a very risky gamble. And they certainly hadn't anticipated anyone arriving upon the scene as quickly as Nicholas must have done. He was suspicious about the time gap from the start, I believe.'

'Do the police know the truth?'

'Yes, we've told them. David has promised to turn over a new leaf, get help with his addiction and I've said I don't wish to press charges. However, the police have said they need to look into it all more thoroughly. You know, the ram-raid with the stolen car and the fact that he had an accomplice, both then and the other night. Caitlin, do you wish to press charges? After all, they inflicted actual bodily harm on you.'

'No, Aunt Jessica, I won't press charges. I just want to forget about it all.'

Caitlin suspected that, whether she pressed charges or not, her young cousin might still find himself serving a spell behind bars but she refrained from confiding these thoughts to her aunt.

'Caitlin, there's something else I want to tell you.' Jessica was looking decidedly sheepish now.

Caitlin wondered wearily what was coming now. She'd had enough revelations confided to her for one day.

'I'm going to sell the gallery and all its contents to Jeremy. It's all been getting on top of me. I realise that now when it's almost too late. I intend to retire and join your parents in the south of France. They've asked me often enough.'

'Have you told Jeremy and Nicholas the truth about David?'

'Yes. Nicholas was threatening all sorts of violence against David at first, for his having sanctioned you being struck down, but Jeremy managed to calm him down.'

She grimaced wryly at Caitlin.

'I think Nicholas is rather fond of you, Caitlin,' and taking no notice of

Caitlin's snort of contempt, went on, 'In fact, they've been very good about it, considering that I've been blaming them for it all. I've been a very silly woman. But then, you realised that all along, didn't you? You were just too sweet natured to tell me so.'

★   ★   ★

There was nothing left to keep Caitlin in Chegston any longer. Her head healed within a few days and she was soon her old self again. As her month was up, there was no legitimate excuse not to return to work. Yet the thought of facing Nicholas, let alone having to work with him was, to say the least, intimidating.

He hadn't been to see her since the supposed break-in and she wondered if, after all, he'd changed his mind about employing her as his assistant after all that had happened between them. Her thoughts returned to the night of the robbery.

When the doctor had finished his examination, it had been Nicholas who had helped her up to bed. David, of course, had insisted on accompanying them. He clearly had mistrusted Nicholas's intentions towards Caitlin.

If Caitlin had been feeling her usual self, she would have smiled to see the two men's obvious dislike of each other. As it was, her head was aching so badly by then, that all she wanted to do was climb into bed.

Nicholas glanced down at the ashen-faced girl when they reached her bedroom. Her head throbbed fiercely and the room began to spin crazily around her. She staggered.

'Steady on.' Nicholas's arm tightened around her. 'Nearly there.'

He sat her gently on the bed, holding her upright with one hand, while, with the other, he tugged back the quilt.

'Right. In you get. Lie down.'

'Nicholas,' she protested weakly, 'I can manage now.'

'In a moment. Let's just get your

dressing-gown off.'

Caitlin raised her hands and held the garment tightly round her. She had no more than a rather skimpy nightdress beneath it.

'Caitlin wants you to go now, can't you see?' David said harshly.

At that, it was as if Nicholas lost patience. He let go of Caitlin and swung round to face David.

'If you don't be quiet, Haydock, I'm going to eject you from the room.'

'Oh, yeah? I'd like to see you try.'

They were the last words Caitlin heard David utter. Nicholas strode across to him, caught hold of him by the back of his shirt collar, and proceeded to do precisely as he'd threatened. He frog-marched David from the room, slamming the door shut behind them both.

Caitlin had the opportunity then to slip out of her dressing-gown and climbed into bed, drawing the cover up. The second she was covered, the door opened again and Nicholas strode in.

What he'd said to David she never discovered but whatever it was, it had the desired effect. She heard her cousin descend the stairs.

'Is everything all right? You haven't hurt him, have you?'

'No,' was Nicholas's unconcerned reply. 'Not yet. But, Caitlin, if I discover that he was behind this evening's events, that young man will have good reason to wish he'd never been born.'

'David! Behind the robbery!' she exclaimed, partially sitting up. 'Don't be ridiculous, Nicholas. Why would he steal from his own mother?'

Nicholas didn't answer, mainly because his thoughts seemed to be taken up with another matter entirely.

'My word, you must have moved quickly.'

His gaze went to the discarded robe lying on the floor at her bedside before it reverted to her almost bare shoulders, now showing over the top of the quilt.

Caitlin slid downward in the bed

again until all that was exposed of her was her head.

'I have seen a woman's body before, Caitlin, you know,' he added quietly. 'There was no need for you to struggle alone.'

Caitlin felt exceedingly foolish. He probably thought her very childish. Nonetheless, nothing would have induced her to be seen by him in such a state of undress! Caitlin felt herself flushing hotly beneath his gaze. But he didn't move, only said, 'Well, if you're sure that you're OK, David's now down in the shop, hopefully erecting some sort of temporary boarding to the smashed window. He's also waiting to reset the alarm system.'

'Oh, right. I'm fine, honestly,' she replied, seeing the frown that lowered his brow as he regarded her hot cheeks.

'Are you? You don't look it.' He put a hand to her brow. 'You look feverish.' But the twitching of his mouth as he suppressed his amusement told her that he knew only too well the reasons for her sudden blush. 'I'll stay if you want, Caitlin.' He glanced around the room. 'I could sleep on that chair.'

'No.' Caitlin spoke quickly. She'd never relax with Nicholas there, watching her. 'I'll be fine, Nicholas. There's no need for that.'

'All right.'

He leaned down and allowed his lips to brush her forehead. Caitlin couldn't repress her sigh or the parting of her lips as she anticipated the longed-for kiss. Nicholas immediately pulled back, letting his gaze rest intently upon her.

He must have read something of her thoughts, for he sat down on the bed and this time, his mouth found hers. It lingered for an endless moment or two, and Caitlin discovered her arms going up round his neck, her fingers sliding into his hair, pulling him closer.

'Don't tempt me, my girl,' he whispered. 'You don't know what forces you'll be unleashing.'

Suddenly Caitlin realised what she was doing, what she was so naively inviting. Quickly, instinctively, she pulled away from him. Nicholas's eyes darkened as he gazed down upon her and his mouth had tightened into an uncompromising line.

'You really are too generous to your men friends, Caitlin.'

Caitlin stiffened, incredulous at the words that he had just ground out. He couldn't mean it, not after kissing her like that, so tenderly. But it was clear that he did. Nicholas was clearly recalling seeing her in Alan's arms the day after he had held her in his own. And now, she had apparently once more welcomed his advances, while, as he thought, she belonged to someone else.

'Damn. Damn. Caitlin, I'm sorry.'

Caitlin said nothing. Then, in a voice that was barely recognisable as her own, muttered, 'Get out, Nicholas.'

She closed her eyes against the hardness of his features. If he wanted to think of her as a cheap, two-timing wanton, then that was up to him. She was too weary to argue.

Once he'd gone, she'd heard the buzz of the burglar alarm being set again and then the soft closing of the shop door and within seconds, Caitlin was sound asleep, exhausted.

* * *

A couple of days after Jessica's return from hospital, Caitlin had been helping her aunt get the larger of the two paintings back into the window and wondering miserably why she'd heard nothing from Nicholas — when he walked into the gallery!

'Caitlin,' he said, then, 'Jessica.'

Jessica took one look at her niece's face and said quickly, 'I'll be upstairs if you want me, Caitlin. We'll finish this later.'

For a moment or two after Jessica had gone, neither Caitlin nor Nicholas said anything. In fact, if she hadn't known him better, Caitlin would have said Nicholas was nervous and uncharacteristically unsure of himself.

As for Caitlin, her heart was racing fit to burst. The memories of the last time she'd been with him, on the night of the robbery, returned to her and her cheeks flamed.

'Hello, Nicholas,' she said, stiffly. 'What can I do for you?'

Her tone was bluntly discourteous but she couldn't seem to help herself. If he'd come to sack her, as she strongly suspected he had, she wasn't going to allow him the satisfaction of seeing her distress.

'I've come to see you,' Nicholas said finally. 'Bruises all gone?'

'Oh, yes,' Caitlin said airily.

'I would have been to see you before.'

'Really.' Caitlin's tone made no secret of her scepticism. 'What for? To find out when I'm coming back to work, or to sack me?'

'Oh, rest assured, I haven't come to sack you, Caitlin. Far from it, actually. I've come to offer you another position.'

'Another position?' Caitlin noticed

that there was a curious calmness to Nicholas. It unnerved her.

To hide her uncertainty, she picked up the duster she'd only just put down and busied herself with the task of cleaning the various prints that were hanging on the walls.

A hand reached out and firmly removed the bright yellow cloth from her grasp, replacing it on a nearby table, before that same hand finally gripped her shaking fingers.

'Do you think you could possibly save the housewife act for later?' Nicholas's voice was low and throaty.

'It's not an act . . . ' But what she saw upon Nicholas's face halted her in mid-sentence.

'Don't you want to know what the position is that's on offer?'

Caitlin shrugged. She seemed to have lost her voice completely.

'I . . . ' The single word was nothing more than a squeak. She tried again. 'I suppose so. Although, I'm surprised you want to offer me anything,

Nicholas, let alone a job.'

Her mutinous expression defied him to answer. Nicholas, being Nicholas, met the challenge that she was offering head-on.

'We'll discuss that later,' he murmured. 'For now, I would rather like to know if you'll accept this special position.'

'Special position?' Against her will, she was intrigued.

'Yes. I've created it just for you, Caitlin.'

His smile conveyed his confidence that she wouldn't be able to resist finding out what he was talking about. She didn't disappoint him.

'Well, go on then. What is this job you're offering?'

'The job of looking after me, Caitlin, personally.' The smile didn't waver.

Caitlin took a deep breath. Did he have to look so complacent? For two pins, she'd turn him down. What did he mean anyway? Look after him, personally?

'But won't I be doing that when I'm your private assistant, Nicholas?'

'Not quite to the extent that I'm envisaging with this new post.'

'Nicholas, will you stop beating around the bush and explain what you mean? I can't say yes or no if I don't know what you're talking about.' Her voice rose, along with her temper.

'OK. I'm asking you to be my wife, Caitlin.'

'What?' She stared aghast. 'Your wife? But — but . . .'

'Yes? But what?' His smile was broadening with every second.

Caitlin looked around wildly. She needed to sit down, before she fell down.

'You can't be serious!' she gasped.

For the second time, Nicholas didn't seem quite so sure of himself. Her response hadn't been what he had expected, that was overwhelmingly evident.

'Well, I hadn't expected you to fling yourself into my arms,' he said drily, 'not immediately, that is. And I suppose I anticipated that it would come as a surprise but I . . . ' His brow wrinkled in a frown. 'Hadn't you suspected anything, Caitlin?' He did sound genuinely astonished.

'Suspect anything?' She eyes him, curiously. 'What should I have suspected?'

'That I'm in love with you, you little idiot.'

Caitlin caught her breath.

'I've loved you since the first time that I saw you. That's why I paid the over-inflated price that Gallagher was asking for his business. I knew it was the only way I was going to get you to spend time with me and perhaps grow to feel the same way as I was doing. Of course, I hadn't anticipated you arriving here in Chegston, all set to enjoy a month's holiday.'

Caitlin expelled her breath slowly, steeling herself to ask the question that had been plaguing her for days now.

'So, why did you say those awful things to me? Make me feel like a — a cheap tramp? I was only responding to something that you had started.'

'Jealousy.' His grin was rueful. 'I was so jealous of that chap, whoever he was. Can you forgive me?'

'Yes. It was someone called Alan,' she answered absently. 'An old boyfriend, no more. But you didn't give me the chance to explain.'

'Would you like to tell me now what you were doing with him that day in the shop?'

'I was trying to fight him off, actually.' It was her turn to speak drily now. 'If you'd been anything of a gentleman, you'd have come to my assistance, not sneaked off and left me to it.'

'What?' Nicholas's expression was one of almost comical horror. 'You mean he was attacking you?'

With two strides, Nicholas reached her. He grasped her by the shoulders.

'What did he do, Caitlin?' His expression was menacing now. 'Tell me.'

'Nothing,' she assured him. 'I made him see the wisdom of leaving before he made a complete ass of himself.'

She smiled up at him and had the immense satisfaction of seeing him draw a long breath.

'Now, about that job offer,' she concluded wickedly. 'If it's still available, I'd like some time to consider it.'

Nicholas's mouth tightened.

'Would you indeed? Two minutes long enough?'

The tiny gold flecks appeared in his eyes. They were a warning to her that he didn't intend being patient for too much longer.

'Just about.'

She fell silent, pretending to turn the matter over.

'Caitlin.' The warning tone induced a mischievous smile.

'Do you know?' His hands tightened upon her as she began to speak. 'I think I just might take you up on your offer, Nicholas.'

She didn't have time to say any more.

Nicholas's patience had finally run out. With a deep-throated growl, he murmured, 'Don't push me too far, my girl. You just might have cause to regret it.'

'Are you threatening me, Nicholas Millward?' Wide, guileless eyes met his.

'Yes, with this.'

The kiss that followed took their breaths away and lingered. When they finally drew apart, they were both quite breathless.

'Oh, Caitlin, I love you so much.'

'I love you, too, Nicholas.'

'At last! I'd begun to think that I was going to have to wring the words out of you.'

'You must have guessed how I felt about you,' she murmured against his cheek.

'Once I came to my senses the night of the burglary, I did have a fair idea, yes. And then I went and almost blew it.'

'Yes, you did,' she agreed.

'My goodness, you don't believe in pulling your punches, do you?'

Nicholas laughed, and Caitlin admired the strong, clean lines of his throat as his head went back.

It was quite amazing. Every one of her preconceptions about him had been turned upon its head. She was stunned by the turn which events had taken. So much so, that she could barely think straight any longer.

'Let's not waste time talking, my darling,' he said softly. 'We've got the rest of our lives for that. For now, I want to hold you, kiss you, love you.' His voice had lowered till it was no more than a husky murmur. 'My father's going to be pleased by all of this. He's been urging me to declare myself for days now.'

'And he's not the only one to be pleased. So am I,' a voice said from just outside of the door.

They swung round together to see Jessica smiling at them both from the doorway.

'You'll have to forgive me! I couldn't help but overhear Nicholas's last few words. I have understood, haven't I? You are getting married.'

Caitlin, breathing a sigh of happiness, nodded.

'Then congratulations, both of you. And welcome to the family, Nicholas.'

'Thank you, Jessica.'

Nicholas let go of Caitlin and took Jessica's outstretched hands in both of his and smiled, firstly at the older woman, and then down at the woman that he was to marry.

'A good way to put all our differences behind us and start a new and happier chapter in the histories of our two families. Don't you agree?'

'I do indeed,' Jessica responded. 'Call your father, Nicholas, and invite him round. Tell him to shut that shop of his for once and I'll open the champagne. This is something to celebrate. The two families are united at last.'

She turned and bustled back upstairs. Nicholas once again folded Caitlin in his arms and kissed her lovingly before picking up the phone. His eyes smiled down into Caitlin's as he lifted the receiver.

Caitlin smiled back at him, blissfully happy at the way things had turned out. For the first time in her life, she felt totally cherished and utterly at peace.

As Aunt Jessica had so rightly said, at last, the two families would be as one. Nicholas squeezed her hand as he began to speak to his father . . .

THE END

FLAMES THAT MELT

Angela Britnell

Tish Carlisle returns from Tennessee to clear out her late father's house in Cornwall — to several surprises. The first is the woman and baby she discovers living there and the second is her father's solicitor, Nico De Burgh, who was Tish's first love. Nico fights their renewed attraction because of a promise made to his foster father but Tish won't give up on him. They must share their secrets before they have any chance of a loving future together . . .

TENDER TAKEOVER

Susan Udy

To Sandy's dismay, she finds herself working for Oliver Carlton, the charismatic man who single-handedly destroyed her family — so when her hatred threatens to turn into something dangerously close to attraction, she uses all of her willpower to fight it. However, it swiftly becomes apparent that Oliver has romantic interests elsewhere, when Sandy catches sight of him with his arm around another woman . . .